Warwickshire County Council

This item is to be returned or renewed before the latest date above. It may be borrowed for a further period if not in demand. **To renew your books:**

- **Phone the 24/7 Renewal Line 01926 499273 or**
- **Visit www.warwickshire.gov.uk/libraries**

Discover • Imagine • Learn • *with libraries*

Warwickshire County Council

Working for Warwickshire

HER LAS VEGAS
WEDDING

HER LAS VEGAS WEDDING

ANDREA BOLTER

MILLS & BOON

First published in Great Britain 2018
by Mills & Boon, an imprint of HarperCollins*Publishers*
1 London Bridge Street, London, SE1 9GF

Large Print edition 2018

© 2018 Andrea Bolter

ISBN: 978-0-263-07396-6

MIX
Paper from
responsible sources
FSC C007454

This book is produced from independently certified FSC™ paper to ensure responsible forest management. For more information visit www.harpercollins.co.uk/green.

Printed and bound in Great Britain
by CPI Group (UK) Ltd, Croydon, CR0 4YY

For Barbara and Moe

CHAPTER ONE

"HERE COMES THE BRIDE." Daniel Girard stood to greet his daughter as she entered his office. Audrey Girard plopped her flight bag down on a chair and gave her dad a peck on the cheek. As both the heiress to the Hotel Girard chain of fine boutique hotels and its director of public relations, she had a slew of things to take care of before their grand opening in Las Vegas. Not the least of which was to organize her wedding.

"When does Reg get in? You probably have more information about my fiancé's schedule than I do," she said. After all, her dad and Reg's father, Connor Murphy, had been planning this marriage between their offspring for the past couple of years. Connor owned the Lolly's chain of casual breakfast eateries that operated in several of the Girard hotels, and the families had been in business together for a decade.

"His flight comes in from LA later this afternoon."

Audrey's intended, Reginald Murphy, was the business half of Murphy Brothers Restaurants. His younger brother, Shane, was the long-haired, mercurial chef. Expanding the Murphy family's interests in the restaurant business, the two brothers had started their own venture. Together, they had crafted the upscale Shane's Table restaurants. After creating a destination dinner spot that was a hit from the moment it opened in New York, they duplicated the success with a second location in Los Angeles. Now they were collaborating with the Girards on this Las Vegas property and hoping Lady Luck would shine upon them here.

"Explain to me again why we're rushing the wedding?" Audrey asked her dad.

"We had never set a date."

"So why now?"

"You've seen the financial statements. We need a big opening for this hotel. A high-profile wedding will really showcase our special-events capabilities."

"So I've got one month to plan the whole thing?"

"We'll make the engagement announcement in two weeks to start generating a buzz."

"When I talked to Reg on the phone a couple of days ago, he didn't sound certain that he was on board with doing the wedding now."

"Connor has concerns about their financial position, as well. The Murphys need this hotel launch as much as we do."

"Gee, I'm glad my future has been reduced to profit and loss statements."

"You know that's not the only reason. Come on now, you're twenty-eight. Reg is, what, thirty-six?"

"You're right, Dad, I'm virtually an old maid."

"You can't blame a couple of fathers for pushing to get their kids to settle down. We want to see you two create a life together. You both work too hard. You should enjoy yourselves. Bring us grandchildren. Not to mention the next generation of hoteliers and restaurateurs."

"Dad, we've talked about that. Children are not in the picture." Not after what Audrey had been through. That was nonnegotiable.

"Never say never."

They moved to the spacious office's reception area, where each sat down on one of armchairs that faced the floor-to-ceiling windows. Audrey took in the view of a couple of the huge hotels and casinos on the Las Vegas Strip, and the majestic red mountains behind them in the distance.

The Hotel Girard Las Vegas sat on a small piece of real estate in between two of the giant monoliths on the Strip. It was originally built in the early 1960s as the Royal Neva Hotel, a sort of bargain casino with one-penny slot machines for visitors who weren't high rollers staying at the big palaces. The lone restaurant had offered two-dollar breakfast specials and the four floors of guest rooms were dirt cheap. The hotel never had the Rat Pack panache of Vegas's heyday, but the architecture was in the midcentury style that defined that era. When it went on sale after closing due to lack of upkeep, the Girards decided to make their first foray in Las Vegas.

With two hundred hotel rooms, as opposed to the three and four thousand of its neighbors, the Girards set out to refurbish the property to appeal to the trend toward boutique hotels, which were their specialty. There'd be no noisy casino. Instead, luxurious suites and amenities, a splendid rooftop pool, unique special-event spaces and exclusive cocktail lounges would provide a chic den for hip guests. The crème de la crème would be Shane's Table, a world-class dining establishment to attract travelers and Vegas locals alike.

Unfortunately, they'd encountered one problem after the next with the project. The original structure was in far worse condition than was initially thought. There had been mold and rot within the walls that required a costly teardown in sections of the hotel. Partial renovations during the years before the Girards bought the property hadn't included solar power or technical upgrades, and energy costs were double what they should have been.

There had been other setbacks to the business, as well, beginning three years ago when Audrey's mother was dying and Daniel was distracted from his duties as CEO.

"I think weddings are going to do it for us at this hotel," Daniel said enthusiastically.

Audrey's business mind agreed. "Special-occasion bookings will bring us a lot of revenue. We have so many great event spaces with this hotel. Showing off the property with a lavish wedding should be publicity gold."

"The marriage of hotel and restaurant royalty will brand the hotel with glamour that will stick in people's minds."

"I had some ideas on the flight here. We can shoot the engagement tea in the garden and a guys' night out at the cigar lounge this week. We'll calendar the press releases and photo spreads to hit after the engagement announcement. No one will know we shot the events ahead of time."

"You and Reg will be an imperial couple. It'll be the romance Las Vegas has always been known for."

Except for the actual romance part, Audrey thought. That was not in her plans. Love was a gamble she wasn't going to bet on. Love involved trust. She'd never fall for that hoax again.

Which is why she had become so contented

with the agreement that she and Reg would wed. Yes, the arranged matrimony felt a bit like something involving territorial feudal kingdoms and armies. Yet, in a different light, having their future spouses decided by their fathers was a smart outsourcing of labor that neither she nor Reg had the time for.

The two were friendly toward each other. They had dinner if they were in the same city, spoke on the phone and had discussed the challenges that their lifestyles would bring to the marriage. With seven Girard hotels throughout the world and a soon-to-be third Shane's Table, they both traveled to and from their businesses almost all of the time and didn't foresee that changing. Reg was a workaholic just like Audrey.

Any comradery they could share would be healthy for her. Currently, she spent what little free time she had by herself. After a childhood where she'd so often been alone, pairing with someone would be a blessing.

She and Reg had concurred that while romantic love was right for some people, it wasn't for them. That compatibility was crucial. What a relief it would be to answer the social pressures to couple off, to find a significant other. There would be no more questions about her dating life from the well-meaning staff at the hotels. She'd always have a companion for events. There might even be shared hobbies and simple dinner-and-movie dates. The list went on.

Most importantly, it was utterly perfect that Reg had zero sex appeal. What Audrey surely didn't need was a man like Reg's brother, chef Shane. A hot-blooded beast who dripped raw power and primitive demands. Reg would never make her pulse flutter like Shane had since the moment she met him. Never cause her to shiver in anticipation of his every move. Never keep her up at night imagining secret pleasures.

"Is Shane on track with his cookbook?" Audrey asked her dad.

"I hear that's not going as smoothly as it should."

She wrinkled her nose, although the information didn't surprise her. With Shane Murphy's bad-boy chef reputation, not to mention his wife's sudden death two years ago, being behind on a deadline would come as no shock.

A peculiar warmth flushed down her neck when she thought of the photo of Shane she'd seen recently on a magazine cover, his almost-black eyes piercing whoever looked at the image. Her reaction to even a photograph of him was involuntary but a little embarrassing, especially as he was to become her brother-in-law. Anything to do with Shane seemed to affect her on a chemical level that she had no control over.

"I'll check into it. Not having the cookbook on schedule could turn into a major problem." Shane Murphy's first cookbook was another essential component of the publicity schedule for the Vegas opening.

"Shane is cooking dinner for you and Reg tonight at the restaurant. You can talk about it then."

Daniel filled his daughter in on the outcome of a meeting he'd had with the human-resources director earlier that day while she'd been on the flight. And about a resolution with a furniture distributor for their hotel in St. Thomas.

Mention of the island brought a wry half smile to Audrey's face with the memory of that weird moment with Shane a decade ago. To this day, the recollection still replayed often in her mind.

It was at the Hotel Girard St. Thomas in the US Virgin Islands that she'd first met the Murphy brothers. When she'd first encountered the volcanic force of nature known as chef Shane Murphy.

Audrey had been a short eighteen-year-old, hiding in baggy shirts because her body hadn't yet settled into its shape. Shane Murphy was the *enfant terrible* of the culinary world at just twenty-four. Reg, the staid older brother at twenty-six. Connor was opening the Lolly's café at the hotel and Shane was there to do a tasting menu in the hotel's formal dining room. The first Shane's Table had already become the hottest dinner reservation in New York, making Shane an instant star.

The two brothers couldn't be more different. Though both were tall, Reg was thin and tidy, save for a perpetually sweaty upper lip. He kept his hair closely cropped and always donned a tailored suit. In contrast Shane's dark curly hair brushed the shoulders of the rock band T-shirts he wore with his jeans. Reg, the immaculate professional, and Shane, the soulful artist. Black and white. Night and day. Shane had made an impression on her that she still carried to this day.

She hadn't seen Shane in person in many months other than through teleconferences, which he would often leave before they were halfway done. Audrey wondered how much his impatience or inattention had to do with the death of his wife two years ago. She knew first-hand how a loss like that could color everything that came after it.

Helping herself to a glass of icy cucumber water from the clear pitcher on the office bureau, she took a much-needed sip. As always seemed to be the case, mere mention of Shane Murphy made Audrey thirsty.

She paced in front of the windows of Daniel's third-floor office. Prior to the renovation, there had only been a couple of picture windows on that exterior wall. With the new sweeping vista she could look out to the hotels and casinos, or peer down to see street-level activity on the al-ways-crowded Strip.

Audrey's eyes fixed on a couple. The young

woman, blonde, short and curvaceous like she was, wore a white minidress and a clip-on bridal veil that looked like it hadn't cost much money. Her groom had on black suit pants and a white shirt with his tie loosened. The two laughed and passed an open bottle of champagne between them to sip from. The bride held her left hand up to the sunlight to admire the ring on her finger. They stopped walking and threw their arms around each other for a passionate kiss.

Las Vegas.

Land of hope. Of gambles. Of chances. Of love.

What would it be like to arrive in Vegas to wed the person you were in love with? Audrey wondered. To embark on a life together, sharing ideas and dreams and romance?

Audrey had no time for thoughts like that. She had her own, practical marriage to plan.

Having made her way from her father's office to the central courtyard of the hotel, Audrey stepped outside into the dry Nevada breeze. The main structure of the building formed a square with a public space in the center with walkthroughs to the Strip and parking so that patrons could enter the restaurants, bars and shops from both inside and outside the building. She was eager to settle into one of the freestanding suites at the back of the property they called the bungalows, where she'd make her home for the time being.

For the past couple of months, she'd been utterly buried by work in her small office at the hotel chain's Philadelphia headquarters. There were splashy incentives to organize and newsworthy stories to cull in order to promote all of the seven hotels for the summer season. Winter had thawed into spring without her really taking note of it.

Along her walk, she said hellos to construction workers and to staff members who were onsite to begin readying the hotel for the opening. This week she'd check in with every department to see what was new and noteworthy that she could use for publicity.

For now, though, she wanted to drop her luggage and check her emails and messages and texts. And see Reg, who had sounded so tentative when she last spoke with him.

As she crossed diagonally through the outdoor public area, she froze on her heels. The Shane's Table restaurant, not yet open for business, appeared to be fully finished, at least on the outside. In front of its door stood a life-sized cardboard cutout photo of chef Shane Murphy.

What the heck?

Audrey was director of public relations and any kind of promotion that went on at Girard hotels came across her desk. It was she who authorized press releases if one of the hotels even so much as bought new towels. If a landscape designer decided on an unusual type of plant for the grounds. When one of the hotels offered a Valentine's Day package that included breakfast in bed.

Yet she'd heard nothing about this horribly tacky six-foot-two-inch shrine to the male ego. What a monstrosity! Not at all befitting the elegance and restraint Girard hotels represented. Nor worthy of the Shane's Table reputation for integrity and excellence.

She didn't know who approved this amateur-hour attempt at marketing for the restaurant. But she was going to find out.

Bustling over, Audrey stopped dead in front of the display. Barely clocking in at five-foot-two herself, she had to crane her neck back to fully study Shane's likeness. The discomfort she always felt in his presence was just as palpable here in this massive photograph.

A wild toss of dark hair seemed to grow from his scalp in every direction as though it belonged on a mythological Medusa. A folded blue bandanna was tied across his forehead and under his hairline. Those black-as-night eyes were framed with long eyelashes and crowned by heavy brows. A straight nose led to full lips, parted slightly, surrounded by beard stubble above his mouth and across his lower cheek and square jaw.

The look on his face was a dare. To say this man was smoldering and dangerous was the understatement of the century. He was almost too much to take in, even in cardboard form. Thank goodness she was marrying safe Reg.

Audrey bit her lip to stay grounded and continue her survey of Shane.

His chef's coat fit well from one broad shoulder to the other. The coat's sleeves were cuffed twice to reveal hefty forearms with a dusting of dark hair. The arms crossed at his chest showcased black leather cording that formed bracelets wrapped around each wrist. One huge hand held a chef's knife.

An embroidered insignia on the chest of the chef's coat depicted his restaurant logo of a four-legged table with the name Shane scripted above it. The coat's hem hit Shane at mid hip, shorter than a typical chef preference. Fitted jeans encased the lower half of his body, with its straight hips and muscular legs. The jeans gave way to black motorcycle boots. One foot crossed over the other in a defiant stance.

Audrey's eyes did a ride up from the boots to the powerfully built chest to the heart-stopping lips. She followed individual locks of jet hair as each made a different wavy descent down around his face.

All she could say to herself was "Whoa!" as that flush swept across her neck again.

Audrey hated cardboard cutout displays that presented a person as some sort of whacked-out Greek statue or national monument. To her, they were a crass and crude form of advertising. But there was no question that Shane Murphy was a drop-dead sexy man. She was painfully aware of it every time she was around him. While it didn't directly have anything to do with his cooking, she wouldn't doubt that his fiery good looks contributed to his restaurants' success.

Nonetheless, Audrey was not about to have that eyesore muddy the sophistication of a Girard hotel. So she lifted cardboard Shane Murphy at his waist, tucked him under her arm and proceeded to her bungalow. As soon as she swiped her key card and let herself in, she propped Shane in a corner of the room facing the bed.

Dropping her bags, she made a three-hundred-sixty degree turn as she took in the finished renovation of the bungalow. The photo and video tours she'd seen didn't do it justice. An interior archway divided the suite into two distinct areas. In the sleeping portion, teal and brown bedding appointed the king bed, a palette that evoked the original sixties style. But a flat-screen smart TV mounted on the wall and tech stations on the two lightwood nightstands brought the room straight into the needs of today's guests. An armchair upholstered in stripes echoed the teal and added in green and cream colors. A reading lamp perched on an end table beside it.

Through the archway, a lightwood desk and chair provided a place to work or eat. Bright abstract paintings adorned the walls. A sitting area with a sleek gray sofa and low coffee table gave way to the sliding-glass door. Each bungalow had a private patio with two forest-green lounge chairs shaded by a partial veranda to give protection against the desert sun.

Audrey delighted at the perfection of the remodel. This was what put the Hotel Girard brand on the map. Everything carefully crafted from fine materials and designs perfectly executed.

Except for that stupid cutout of Shane Murphy, of course.

"There he is." Daniel nudged Audrey as they sat in a finished section of one of the hotel's cocktail lounges.

They both stood as Reg Murphy approached. Audrey's future husband was a slim man who stood ramrod straight. He wore a three-piece pinstriped suit. Audrey couldn't remember the last time she saw a man wear a vested suit.

She hadn't had a chance to unpack but had pulled an outfit from her garment bag for the evening. A conservative gray sheath dress and black sandals.

"Nice to see you, Reg."

"I guess this is finally it," he said as he extended his right hand as if to shake hers. Then he seemed to change his mind midstream and instead lifted her hand and turned it over to kiss the back of it. His supple palm pressed her fingers against his open lips. The whole maneuver was awkward and a bit moist.

"How was your flight?" Daniel asked as Reg vigorously shook his hand up and down.

"Fine, sir."

Audrey remembered Reg as being a bit more poised. Perhaps it was wedding jitters that made him appear so nervous. He stared at Daniel slack-jawed like he wanted to say something, but instead pulled a white handkerchief out of his jacket pocket and dabbed his upper lip.

"Are you in Vegas now until the opening?" Audrey asked.

"I may have to fly back to New York. You?"

"Yeah, I'm here. I've got our wedding to co-ordinate."

"Right." Reg nodded as if it were just sinking in. He glanced at his phone and read something on the screen that brought a huge smile to his lips. "Please pardon me a moment while I return this message."

He tapped onto the screen, grinning the entire time.

"Well," Daniel said using his right hand to pat Audrey's back and his left to tap Reg's, "I'll leave you two to your evening."

"Thanks, Dad."

After Daniel walked away, Reg and Audrey each perched on a stool beside the table. One of the four bars on the property, this space was located inside the main lobby and had stylish fun in mind. The decor was done with white barstools upholstered in deep purple velvet set around chrome pedestal tables. Behind the chrome cocktail bar was a giant glass tank filled with undulating purple goo similar to the lava lamps of the 1960s.

Once again, Girard's interior designers had worked through an idea to perfection. And then capable crews were able to bring the vision to fruition. Audrey could imagine the lounge with chic music playing in the background and filled with trendy patrons choosing drinks from a cocktail menu that offered libations with names like *Flip-Out Frappe* and *Yin-Yang-Yum.*

"After all of the talk about us marrying, this has come about rather suddenly, hasn't it?" Reg asked.

"Is there a problem with that?"

He seemed to be a million miles away. "Not at all."

"I think the extra push makes sense. Do everything at once. Open the hotel and Shane's Table. Shane's cookbook. Our marriage. It's a cascade of publicity on several levels."

Audrey knew that the Girard hotels had never really recovered from the events of three years ago. When her mother was dying and her father was unable to concentrate on the business. Audrey had tried as best she could to fill in for him. It was a gift to have the work to focus on since her mother hadn't wanted her at her bedside.

All of her life, it had been assumed that she'd grow up into the family business. As a teenager, she developed a knack for coming up with advertising ideas and events. The marketing side of the brand was a perfect fit for her after college.

Hotel Girard Incorporated was Audrey's entire world. Running around the properties as a kid, she had known every secret passageway. Every painting that hung in every guest room. Every item sold in the gift shops. Any happiness she could recollect took place within the borders of the hotels. The staff were loyal to Audrey and she was loyal to them. She'd do anything needed for their good. Even get married.

Besides, she thought Reg was a good match and she had become quite amenable to the marriage idea. He was smart. Nice-looking, too. Maybe a little too much hair product. Those short curls might look better if they weren't so stiff. He was poised and polite and she didn't know what the medical condition was that made a person have a sweaty upper lip but, hey, she thought she could overlook that.

And he was, safely, nothing like his brother. That split second ten years ago on St. Thomas flickered in her mind again. A freeze-frame in time that she still secretly compared every-thing else to.

"Should we go to dinner?" she asked. Reg seemed so uneasy tonight, perhaps a change of atmosphere would help. Devotion to the hotels was one thing but she wasn't going to go as far as to beg him to wed her if he didn't want to.

"Shane is cooking for us in the restaurant." Reg took Audrey by the bony part of her elbow and lead her out of the bar. "We are essentially the first guests at Shane's Table Las Vegas."

Along the way, Reg stopped to read and re-spond to another message on his phone. The same amusement that had come across his face earlier returned while he typed.

But he hesitated when they reached the res-taurant's entrance. "Where is the display that's supposed to be here?"

"You mean that awful stand-up photo of Shane?"

"Name recognition is what Shane's Table is all about."

"I'm well aware of that. But that cardboard cutout was absurd. Brash advertising like that is not how Girard maintains its reputation for taste and understatement."

Not that a life-size photo of hottie Shane Murphy was hard on the eyes, but it was, nonetheless, inconsistent with the Girard style.

"You personally removed my advertising?"

She'd stood it up in her bungalow for the time being and now didn't seem the right time to confess that. "Reg, I'm head of public relations. I work alongside a marketing team and together we decide when and how best to…"

"I built Shane's Table into what it is today."

Wow, Audrey wasn't expecting this. She assumed Reg would respect her authority on this topic. He should have at least proposed the display prior to just having it planted it in front of the restaurant's doors, which was technically Girard property.

Audrey attempted to smooth ruffled feathers. "You know, Reg, perhaps I'm not a hundred percent clear on what our contracts state about my role concerning the PR specifically for the restaurant."

"I'll have my lawyers call yours in the morning."

She stroked his thin arm once up and once down in a gesture of calming affection. "That's a great idea. Can we just put the issue aside for now and enjoy our dinner? I can't wait to see the completed dining room."

The pacifying technique worked because Reg pulled from his pocket a deadbolt key and an access fob to open the front door of the newly finished construction. He reached to flick on a temporary lamp that stood just inside the entrance.

Rock 'n' roll blared from the far end of the restaurant. Reg gestured for Audrey to follow him across the dark dining room and through the double doors leading into the kitchen.

The lone man in the cavernous space stood with his back facing them, but Audrey easily recognized that long curly hair and the broad shoulders that filled out his chef's coat. The music was turned up so loud that he hadn't noticed anyone had entered. His head bobbed and his hips ground to the beat as he sautéed something smoking hot on the stove in front of him. Reaching for a spoon, he tasted from the pan.

"Garbage," he decreed and, in frustration, threw the spoon into the nearby sink.

Only then did he turn enough to be startled by Reg and Audrey's presence. He grimaced. His gorgeous full lips twisted. A pulse beat in his neck. His eyes locked on Audrey.

"Audrey," Reg yelled above the music, "you remember my brother, Shane Murphy."

CHAPTER TWO

"HI, SHANE," Audrey said, turning on the polish. In reality, his intense stare made her heart skip every other beat. "Can you believe it was a full year ago when we stood right here after the old restaurant had been gutted?"

Shane slowly, sinfully, with no restraint whatsoever, inventoried her. From the part in her blond hair, across her face, down every curve of her fitted dress and shapely legs, through her sandals to the tips of her orange-painted toes.

Her legs twitched from his gaze.

He mashed his lips together as he shifted something internally and turned his attention to his brother. "I mixed a white sangria and put it on the bar. Why don't you take Audrey into the dining room and pour it, Reg?"

"Join us for a glass, won't you?"

Unspoken communication passed between the two brothers.

"I'll be out with some appetizers in a few minutes."

Reg ushered Audrey out of the kitchen and turned on the overhead lighting.

The restaurant was a showstopper. One entire wall made of glass looked out to a furnished patio. A wood-burning oven, large grill and two fire pits would allow for al fresco cooking. The open-air space was enclosed by a semi-circular wall made of small stones. At three points, waterfalls rained down. The effect was that of a private outdoor world far from the bright lights of Las Vegas.

Inside, shaded lighting fixtures hung from the ceiling to cast a play of light and shadow throughout the room. Tall-backed chairs cushioned in an olive-colored fabric, teakwood tables and booths dotted the dining room, each placed with enough space between them to allow for dinner conversation. Carpeting in a subtle diamond pattern of khaki and red would muffle the din of a full house. Stone tiling on the walls gave the room a lodge feel that was posh but comfortable.

Audrey took her time inspecting it all. "Everything turned out spectacularly."

Reg guided Audrey by the tip of her elbow again, a trend she wasn't enjoying, to the one table in the center of the dining room that had been set for dinner.

"I'll get the wine," he said as he pulled out one of the chairs for her. Then he hopped down the three steps to the bar to retrieve a carafe. "Shane used a 2009 pinot gris from the local Desert Castle vineyard we're working with," Reg announced as he poured each of them a glass. Crisp green apple slices and chunks of fresh peaches floated in the drink.

"Nice," Audrey said after a quick sip, never one to drink much alcohol. Not after what she had witnessed. "You're staying in a condo in Vegas?"

"In the Henderson suburb. I suppose when the two of us…" Reg stopped, seemingly at a total loss of how to complete the sentence. "Shane leases a flat behind the Strip," he added and ran the back of his index finger under his nose.

"Will he base himself mostly in Vegas?"

"For a while. When we first opened in Los

Angeles, it took a year until we were functioning smoothly."

"It takes a long time to build a core staff that you feel confident in. People don't work out. You hire new ones."

"Shane is very exacting in what he expects. As you'll recall."

A flush of heat spread down Audrey's neck.

"Ten years was a long time ago." Audrey made reference to the St. Thomas collaboration. "I was just starting college so I wasn't really involved, but I do have a vague memory," she fibbed when, in fact, she remembered every second of that summer.

The twenty-four-year-old wunderkind chef and his demands in the kitchen had been legendary. "Didn't the controversy begin with some herb we couldn't get onto the island?"

"I still don't know how I was supposed to make a yellow mole without hoja santa." Shane's thick vibrato filled the dining room. Audrey didn't know how they had failed to hear him come out from the kitchen.

The surprise sent a blush all the way under the neckline of her dress.

"And your idiot sous chef suggested I use cilantro."

"I was all of eighteen so, believe me, I was just an innocent bystander at the time."

"We were on a tiny island, Shane." Reg lifted his palms. "They weren't able to fly in your herb."

Shane held two small plates. Audrey took notice of the black leather cords he had roped around his wrists like the ones he wore in the cardboard cutout. There was something so rebellious about them. She'd never known a chef to wear jewelry on his hands. Yet she found them as mysterious and exciting as the man who donned them. His hands were so massive they made the dishes of food he carried look tiny.

"Nevada appears to be the motherlode for the ingredients I need," Shane said as he placed one plate in front of each of them. "Chiles en nogada. Poblano stuffed with pork, pear and mango and topped with a walnut cream sauce."

Audrey's eyes widened at the striking presentation on the plate. She knew that the sprinkle of diced red and green peppers on top of the white sauce was in homage to the colors of the Mexican flag. The foundation of Shane Murphy's menus was in the flavors of the Spanish-speaking world.

While Shane waited intently, she took a bite, careful to get a little morsel of each ingredient onto her fork. The rich cream fragrant with ground walnuts brought a decadent lushness to the pork, yet the dots of fruit kept the dish from being too heavy.

Audrey closed her eyes to savor the combination.

Depriving herself of sight, she could sense even more powerfully how Shane's eyes bored into her face. Making her feel somehow exposed and beautiful at the same time.

She whispered upon opening her eyes and looking at Shane again, "Magnificent." Possibly in reference to the food.

Shane pulled a fork out of the back pocket of his jeans and showed it to Reg. "There was a mistake with the order that came in today. Three tines? Am I serving Neanderthals?"

Without another word, Shane turned and returned to the kitchen.

Audrey noticed the four tines on the fork she was holding. She appreciated how important every small decision was for these consummate professionals. It was the same level of concern the Girards applied to their hotels.

"Audrey, I need to talk to you."

They were only on the appetizer and she was already feeling unfocused and exhausted from being around Shane. Reg had just said something, but she hadn't really heard him. "Has Shane always been so—" she chose her word "—fierce?" Although she guessed the answer.

"Since the day he was born." Reg shook his head. "Our grandmother Lolly, who taught him how to cook her old Irish recipes, used to call him Mr. Firecracker. Of course, since Melina died he's been grappling with his own demons. Forks are the least of his problems."

The loss of his wife had left behind a wounded ogre. Audrey knew the story. The young woman who had been killed instantly in a car accident during a snowstorm in the woods of upstate New York. She hadn't seen the Murphys very often during that time period, but her dad had sent flowers and reached out to Connor to offer his support.

Audrey asked Reg, "Does Shane talk about her?"

Reg dabbed under his nose and sounded exasperated when he questioned, "Why are we spending so much time discussing Shane?"

In his kitchen, Shane took out his frustration on the mint he tore for the salad. With a syncopated rhythm, he ripped leaves from their stems and threw them onto a work board. His preferred soundtrack of hard rock music did little to squelch the thoughts stomping through his head.

When he'd first heard this master scheme of Audrey Girard being matched up with his brother, he heartily approved. Reg spent far too much time agonizing over spreadsheets, finding fault with staff members and riding Shane about the cookbook or the lagging business. Hopefully a wife would take up some of Reg's attention and get him off of everyone else's back.

But now, face-to-face with Audrey again, the whole idea angered him. Wasn't she just a little too pretty, a lot too sexy and even a bit too in-dependent to be with uptight Reg? He loved his brother and wanted the best for him, but Au-drey was too fine a lamb to be offered up for this sacrifice.

During the meetings regarding the new res-taurant, he'd observed petite but voluptuous Audrey Girard in action. In her tight business skirts, she moved with the charged-up energy to match the clack of her high-heeled shoes. In fact, memories of her would linger in his mind for days after every encounter.

While Shane wielded his knife to halve the cherry tomatoes, a tight smile crossed his lips. He remembered the first time he'd met Audrey, still in her teens back then, during that summer in St. Thomas when he was doing a promotional stint as a guest chef.

She had been scared to death of him. Who could blame her? At twenty-four, with his heavy boots and impossible standards, he must have cut a frightening figure. Another sneer broke through as he realized that not much had changed since then.

Except for two massively successful restaurants that had made his name a household word. Although the world didn't know that the restaurants had ceased making the profits they used to. Had anyone noticed that he was no longer asked to make appearances on national morning TV talk shows? That the public had moved on to new culinary revelations, new rising-star chefs? One thing they did know was that Shane Murphy had lost his wife to a gruesome death.

He plated the tomatoes and crumbled cojita cheese on them. Yes, he still remembered Audrey Girard and that midnight ocean swim. He flicked the mint on top of the cheese. Drizzled on olive oil and finished with a dotting of manzanilla olives. He could do this salad in his sleep.

All afternoon, he had been alone in the kitchen, trying to come up with a fresh idea. Just one new recipe for the cookbook. A start.

But he'd only spun his wheels. Unable to summon a clear vision. Nothing was right.

A muse was nowhere to be found.

"Aha," Shane heard Reg call out as he entered the dining room with the salads he'd served tens of thousands of in his restaurants. "We were just talking about the cookbook."

"What about it?" Shane already knew where this conversation was going.

"That perhaps we'll shoot some photos of you on the patio," Reg said. "Fire up the grill out there, and you can do street tacos with a party crowd surrounding you."

Shane placed the salad plates on an empty table nearby so that he could clear Reg and Audrey's appetizers away before serving. Audrey had only eaten a few bites of the poblano.

"You didn't like it," he announced rather than inquired.

Audrey looked up at him with her big eyes. He hadn't remembered how light a brown they were. The color of honey. "It was delicious," she answered, as if she thought that was something she needed to say.

"I see."

Shane kept his connection with Audrey's seductive orbs while Reg asked, "Are you any closer to actually finishing the cookbook, brother? Or even beginning it?"

"Enjoy the salad," Shane uttered between clenched teeth.

Back in the kitchen, he dialed up his music even louder.

Even if he didn't like it, he could see how the pairing of Reg and Audrey would benefit business. That was an important consideration now that Murphy Brothers Restaurants needed to take a huge step forward. A soaring success here could lead to more Shane's Table restaurants in other Girard hotels.

Shane rocked his hips to the beat of a heavy metal song as he deveined the shrimp for the Guatemalan tapado.

And let's face it, his brother needed to get married. A woman's touch was going to be the only way to get Reg to lighten up. Plus their parents, now semiretired, longed for grandchildren. Shane would never marry again or have children. Reg was their only hope.

His dad and Daniel Girard used to joke around about matchmaking Reg and Audrey, but after Melina's death the talk became serious. Shane had made an impulsive marriage that ended in disaster. His father probably felt he needed to step in to insure his other son had a more controllable fate.

After a hand wash, Shane began sautéing the onions and peppers.

One marriage was quite enough for Shane, thank you very much. He was clearly not to be trusted with the well-being of another person. Not a day went by that he didn't think about the death that maybe he could have prevented. Had he been a different person. In fairness if Melina had been, too.

Shane added the coconut milk that was the basis of the sauce to the sauté pan. Mixed in a ladleful of stock. Stirred in his seasonings.

If a Murphy brother was to marry, it was definitely going to be Reg.

Then why did he picture Audrey, with those spectacular golden eyes smiling at him, while a voice to the side of them asked, "Shane Niall Murphy, do you take this woman…?" Why was he picturing lifting a white-dressed Audrey up into his arms and carrying her over a doorway threshold into a private suite?

Tossing the shrimp into his sauce, he reckoned that the prospect of anyone getting married probably brought up twisted wedding images for him. He was just having a distorted waking nightmare about Melina.

Swirling in a handful of chopped chard, he finished the dish. He portioned cooked rice onto two plates and spooned his stew on top of each. Another recipe he could cook with his eyes closed.

Coming out from the kitchen with his tapado de camaron, Shane noticed from twenty feet away that Audrey hadn't finished her salad. Was she one of *those* girls, who only pecked at food? He'd always noticed the seriously lush curves on that small frame of hers. She didn't look like a bird who didn't eat.

Were his flavors too unusual for her? Was she used to a blander palate?

He placed the dinner dishes down on the side table.

"You didn't like the salad, either." He hastily snatched Audrey's barely touched plate. "I sell a lot of them."

"It was lovely, I'm just not that hungry," Audrey sputtered like she was making an excuse.

Shane served his entrée.

"Have a seat with us," Reg instructed, gesturing for Shane to pull a chair over from one of the other tables. Reg refilled his own sangria glass and slid it into position for Shane to have it. Audrey's was barely touched.

For all of his brother's annoyances, Shane respected Reg more than anyone in the world. Reg had provided the necessary foresight and know-how to lift Shane's Table to fame. Shane could never have done any of it without him.

Reg had taught him that he had to play the game sometimes, had to make nice with people even when he'd rather be hiding in the kitchen. So he obeyed his brother, turned around a chair and straddled it backward to sit down with them.

"We need to have a discussion about the cookbook," Reg said with a concerned look. Had they been spending the whole dinner talking about him? "You know we've committed to a date with the publisher and they, in turn, agreed to create a mock-up so we can do marketing with it."

"If it's a mock-up, then it could be filled with empty pages—what's the difference?"

"Because you have a contract with them, saying that you're going to deliver a cookbook," Audrey added. "They're not going to go forward if you're not going to meet the deadline."

"The TV taping is going to bring you and the restaurant into the living room of millions of viewers," Reg said.

"We'll not only sell cookbooks," Audrey said, "but it will bring people to Vegas to eat at Shane's Table."

"You know we all need this," his brother added.

"The publicity could put us at capacity for a year," Audrey stressed.

Reg and Audrey both paused to take bites of their tapado. Reg gestured his approval while Audrey stayed straight-faced and chewed slowly. Reg asked, "Have you even started it?"

"Enough already. I get it. I have to deliver the cookbook." With that, Shane hitched up from the chair and stomped back into the kitchen.

Annoyed, he portioned the pastel de tres leches he had made this afternoon. He hated being ganged up on like that. Hated all of that aggressive sales-y behavior, even though he knew that was what it took to be successful. Just as he knew he wasn't at all cut out for it. And as for that smart-talking bombshell Audrey... He'd like to show her how actions spoke louder than words.

Shane, he reprimanded himself, *Audrey is going to be your sister-in-law. You do not kiss your sister-in-law. You do not even think about kissing your sister-in-law. For heaven's sake.*

Yet he lingered on a mental image of feeding her something delicious with his fingers.

After he and rock 'n' roll had cleaned up the kitchen, he'd blown off enough steam to go serve the pastel.

Assuming this would be the fourth dish Audrey picked at but didn't finish, he placed the plate in front of her without much enthusiasm even though he knew this dessert was always a hit.

She gawked at the cake. Took a small forkful. As she slipped it between lips that were as juicy as the plums Shane'd had for breakfast that morning, he could swear he saw her eyelashes flutter. After her bite, she managed, "Wow."

"It's called tres leches because it's got condensed milk, evaporated milk and cream," he said of the sponge cake soaked in the custardy milk mixture and topped with whipped cream to make it even richer.

She took another demure forkful. Which was quickly followed with another, not as ladylike in size as the previous. Both Shane and Reg couldn't help but watch as she devoured one bite after the next.

The three chitchatted a bit about a successful New York bakery chain and how they went about their expansion.

Shane hadn't seen Reg in a couple of weeks. Something more than his usual worries was bothering him. He'd thought his brother had been in favor of this friendly marriage to Audrey. Maybe something had changed. He needed to speak with him privately.

But in between snippets of conversation, Audrey took bite after bite of the cake. Until it was gone. She made a final swirl around the plate with her fork to capture any bits that might have been left behind.

Then she pointed to Reg's plate. "Are you going to finish yours?"

Gotcha! A pirate grin slashed across Shane's mouth. After she'd barely eaten the dinner, he finally had her. "Now we see what you like, Sugar."

Audrey swiped the key card to her bungalow, opened the door and immediately eyed the cardboard cutout of Shane she had removed from the restaurant entrance earlier. "What are you looking at?" she snapped at the photo, which seemed to have a raised eyebrow she didn't remember from earlier.

No sooner had she arrived in Vegas than three handsome men had overwhelmed her. One was her father. She knew Daniel wanted the best for her and his concern for her unmarried status was at least half of his motivation in the matchmaking. Two tall, dark and handsome brothers were the other players.

The idea of a marriage being arranged and handed to her in a neat organized file was a relief. At twenty-eight, she knew she had decades of work ahead of her to keep up the Girard legacy that her father, and his father before him, had worked so hard to build. Yet she knew that going it completely alone could be a hard path.

A distant and uncaring mother had cured her of any silly dreams about a love that takes a whole heart. She would never set herself up for that kind of hurt again. Words like *allegiance* and *devotion* had been removed from her dictionary. *Sensible* and *logical* were welcome.

Timing the wedding to coincide with the opening was a good move. Audrey hoped Reg felt the same way. He had never gotten around to telling her what he wanted to talk to her about tonight, partially because he became invisible every time his brother burst into the dining room.

Shane was a thunderstorm of a man, all mysterious dark skies and punishing rain. Obviously still not over the death of his wife, he hulked under a cloud. That obsession with what she was, and wasn't, eating had been so annoying. Audrey snarked at the photo of him in the corner. How smug he had become when she couldn't stop eating that unbelievably scrumptious tres leches cake.

Throwing one of her suitcases up on the bed, she started to unpack as she hadn't had time to earlier. In a month she'd be married to Reg. There was no reason to care what the other Murphy brother thought of her. Yet when she unzipped the interior, she almost convinced herself that she had to open the flap in a direction that blocked Shane's photo from seeing what was inside. Was she crazy?

Okay, Shane. Here it is, she thought defensively as she pulled the first item from the case. Cookies. Yes, she had brought package upon package of her favorite cookies from Philadelphia! She didn't know if they would carry them in Vegas stores so she had stuffed as many as she could into her luggage. And not just cookies. There were boxes of candy from a famous Philadelphia chocolatier, too. There was no way she could live without those. When she ran out, she'd order more online.

"I like sweets. So what?" she challenged Shane's disapproving expression. He had no business becoming the third man prying into her affairs. She should just get that six feet and two inches of cardboard out of the bungalow tonight and be done with it. Hopefully Reg would ask for it tomorrow.

Yet somehow she liked it right where it was. Those deep, dark eyes of Shane's were magnets that pulled her in and wouldn't let go. She wanted to dive into those eyes, to understand the complexity, agony and secrets she knew lay beneath them. As nice as the furnishings in the suite were, Shane was clearly the focal point.

Once she emptied her suitcases, she picked out a nightgown and went to change in the bathroom so as not to let Shane's photo see her naked. *Bonkers*, she confirmed to herself, but did it anyway.

After she pulled back the covers on the bed and climbed in, she realized she wasn't the slightest bit tired. So she didn't turn off the bedside lamp. She examined Shane's full lips. Wondered how that beard stubble would feel against the delicate skin of her neck. Scratchy and rough in the most divine way, she figured. And she pondered his tangle of dark hair, the snug fit of his jeans, those leather cord bracelets!

No, Audrey didn't lie down and go to sleep.

Instead, she bolstered up her pillows. Leaned back and laced her fingers behind her head.

She was going to win this staredown with Shane.

Even if it took all night.

Shane leaned back against one of the archways in the wedding pavilion, an outdoor terrace space shaded by an awning and edged by long rectangular planters filled with desert succulents. The late afternoon sun had moved toward the mountains and he crossed one leg over the other and folded his arms across his chest to settle in for a gander at the spectacle at hand. The pain-in-the-behind photographer who had just tortured him through a session in the restaurant was now at work on Audrey and Reg.

The guy and his assistant buzzed around like bees. Positioning Reg's hand a couple of inches higher, repinning one lock of Audrey's glossy hair, patting Reg's face with a cloth.

Shane didn't like the way Audrey was fashioned today. Was that some stylist's idea of the blushing bride to be? The updo hair was far too prim for someone as sexy as Audrey. The floral-print dress and pink shoes looked too coun-try club. That sweet image was pretty on some women. But it just wasn't Audrey. He wanted to smear that pink lipstick right off of her mouth.

He chuckled to himself as the bees swarmed around the happy couple, posing them this way or that. If it was up to him, he would have Au-drey in a bloodred dress cut way down to there, fitted enough to hug every one of her tempt-ing curves. He'd leave that exquisite blond hair unfastened and free. And he wouldn't allow a speck of makeup to come between her smooth-ness and his hands or mouth.

There he went again, conjuring up improper images about the woman who was betrothed to his brother! And even if she wasn't, he was never going to marry again so he didn't need to be fantasizing about what his fiancée would wear in their engagement photos. Ridiculous.

Daniel Girard appeared from the other end of the pavilion nicely dressed in a beige suit.

Shane had on his signature chef's coat and jeans.

"Daniel, Shane, we're ready to bring you in for a couple of shots," the head bee called.

With a roll of the eyes, Shane trudged over. The Murphy brothers with their partners in business, and now in life, the Girards. Shane was apparently about to become Audrey's brother-in-law.

He had burned the few photos of him and Melina that they had taken the day they went to a justice of the peace in New York to become a legally married couple. It had been a no-fuss ceremony. Afterward, they'd had lunch with Reg, Shane's parents and Melina's mother. Melina's estranged father was not in attendance.

When he looked back on it, Shane wasn't really sure why he had agreed to marry Melina. It was she who'd wanted to. As a young man with the level of fame the restaurants brought, Shane attracted more than his fair share of chef groupies. He supposed Melina pressured him into marriage to try to insure his fidelity. The truth was that he'd been so immersed in cooking and the restaurants at that point, she needn't have worried. Though he did seek acclaim, he had no interest in sexual dalliances.

Melina was an outcast blueblood. Her father, a wildly successful mogul overseas, had cut her off because of her party lifestyle, but that hadn't changed her ways. Shane met her at an art gallery opening after he had returned to New York once the LA restaurant was up and running.

She was an eccentric who sang in a band. As a young star chef, Shane had temporarily enjoyed the diversion of her rock 'n' roll crowd, who were in great contrast to the luminaries of New York who came into the restaurant.

But he'd tired of the superficiality of Melina's orbit. And had become acutely aware that they were not growing closer. They were not turning marriage into a foundation to stand on together. Their apartment was not a home.

It had been a reckless and immature decision to marry Melina. Even their nuptials were a spur-of-the-moment plan on a Tuesday afternoon. They had never been right together.

His four years with her were now comingled with memories regarding the horror of her death. The phone call from the highway patrol. Police officers who were gracious enough to come to the cabin to pick him up during the snowstorm and drive him to identify his wife's body.

Shane hadn't even been a guest at a wedding

in many years, so he'd forgotten about all of the pomplike engagement photos. Now, the next wedding he'd attend would be his brother's. Studying Audrey again, whose mere being seemed to light something buried down inside of him, he simply couldn't picture her and his brother together.

Reg seemed ill at ease with this photo shoot, breaking frequently to text. They hadn't had a chance to talk privately last night, but Shane could tell his brother was bearing the weight of the world on his slim shoulders.

After the last photos were taken and the bees left, Reg's phone rang and he took the call. Shane didn't like the look of alarm that came over his face. "Rick in New York." Reg identified the caller. "Shane, take Audrey into the kitchen and show her the progress you've made on the cookbook so far."

"Alright, let's go." Shane took Audrey by her hand, which was even tinier and softer than he'd imagined it was going to be, and tugged her in his direction. There wasn't much to show her but maybe it was time he assessed what he had.

In the restaurant kitchen, Shane rifled through

the papers on his desk, all of which needed his attention. From under them he pulled a tattered manila folder. He dumped its contents onto a countertop.

Audrey looked surprised but managed a pursed lip.

"This is how I work," he said.

Ideas for recipes were written on food-stained pieces of paper. On napkins where the ink had smeared. On sticky notes that were stuck together. On the backs of packing slips from food deliveries. On shards of cardboard he'd torn from a box. There was one written on a section of a dirty apron.

"O...kay," Audrey prompted, "tell me exactly what's here."

He glanced down to the front of the floral dress she was wearing for the photo shoot. The pattern of the fabric was relentless in its repetition of pink, yellow and orange flowers. Begonias, if he had to guess. The way she filled out the dress sent his mind wondering about what sweet scents and earthly miracles he might find beneath the thin material.

Shane wanted to know what was under the

dress, both literally and figuratively. She was an accomplished woman yet he thought there was something untouched and undernurtured in her.

He admonished himself for again thinking of his brother's soon-to-be bride, although he took a strange reassurance in the fact that this was an arranged marriage between people who were not in love.

Still, it was nothing he had any business getting involved in.

What he needed to concentrate on were these scraps of paper that were to become one of those sleek and expensive cookbooks that people laid on their coffee table as a design accessory and never cooked from. A book whose pages held close-up pictures of glistening grapes and of Shane tossing a skillet of wild mushrooms.

"These are my notes." A scrap from the pile caught his eye. "Feijoada."

He'd scribbled that idea over a year ago. When Reg had asked him to think about how to make use of the lesser cuts of pork he had left over from other recipes. "I've seen Brazilians throw everything into this stew, the ears, the snout, all of it. The whole pot simmers with the black beans for a long time and you squeeze the flavor out of every morsel."

"Let's see what you have," Audrey offered. She leaned close to him to read the note together.

His tendons tightened at the sweet smell of her hair.

"There are no amounts for the ingredients," she observed.

"Obviously."

"How are we going to use these notes for recipes then?"

"I have no idea."

"How do you get the dishes to taste the same every time if you don't have the measurements written down?"

"I feel it. They don't come out exactly the same every time."

"You feel it." She bit her lip. "Then how would someone at home be able to cook them?"

"They wouldn't."

Shane watched Audrey's expression go from irritated to intelligent as she thought through what she should say next. "You're not at Shane's Table in New York and Los Angeles cooking every single dish. How does your staff prepare the food?"

"Of course the restaurant menu recipes are written down. We'll use a few Shane's Table guest favorites for the book. But it's supposed to be all new food. Reg promised we'd deliver fresh, rustic and regional, and I'm still working on the dishes. The measurements are the least of my problems."

Audrey took a big breath into her lungs and held it there.

She sure looked adorable when she was thinking.

"I'm trying to work with you here, Shane." She exhaled. He liked hearing her say his name. "The restaurant menu had to have been ideas in your head at the beginning. How did you develop the recipes for those?"

"That was a long time ago." Before Melina died. Before grief and frustration and anger clouded his mind and heart. Nowadays he went through the motions but stayed under the darkness. Which was how he wanted it. Or thought he did anyway.

Another Shane's Table was opening. Truthfully, so what? A cookbook as a publicity stunt Reg said would bring their brand to every corner of the world. So what? The Feed U Project with the kids was about all he cared about anymore. Just as he and his family had done in a dozen other locations, he'd turned a warehouse in downtown Vegas into a kitchen where he taught local kids how to cook.

Reg's call interrupted his musing. His brother wanted to meet right away.

"I gotta go, Sugar," he said to the five-foot-two ray of light.

"I thought we were supposed to achieve something on the cookbook today."

He turned to the pan he had cooling on a nearby rack. With his fingers, he broke off a taste of what he had baked earlier. From an old recipe that it had occurred to him to whip up this morning. With Audrey in mind, if he was being honest.

"Pan de dulce de leche. Caramel." Shane popped the chunk of still-warm cake into her delectable mouth.

CHAPTER THREE

"IT'S BAD," Reg told Shane as they reached the edge of the pool after a lap. "Much worse than we thought."

"Kitchen or front-of-the-house kind of worse?" Shane knew the New York and Los Angeles restaurants weren't making the profits they once were but, apparently, that wasn't the extent of it.

He shook some water from his hair.

When Reg had called while he was in the kitchen with Audrey half an hour ago, Shane suggested they meet for a swim in the employee pool. The Girards made a practice of building a private pool or gym at all of their hotels exclusively for the employees to enjoy. Though this pool was small and not at all like the deluxe rooftop pool area for guests, it was a handy, gated-off oasis that Shane had taken to using often.

"Both kinds of worse," Reg continued his report. Shane could tell from the tone in his brother's voice that this wasn't just going to be "the price of tablecloths went up" bad.

"What?"

"Lee quit." Their executive chef in New York. The man they had left in charge of running the kitchen while they kept their eye on LA and put their energies into getting this third restaurant off the ground.

Shane's jaw flexed in disbelief. "Why?"

He'd always had a good relationship with Lee, whose friendly disposition never wavered no matter how difficult Shane could be.

"He got a better offer. A full partnership in London. Doing Korean food."

Shane sighed. "That's what he always wanted."

"Effective immediately," Reg added.

"Effective immediately?"

"I don't have a lot of the details," Reg continued. "He apologized profusely. Said he'd call you."

"No executive chef in New York." This was devastating. Shane couldn't be in three places at once. He'd counted on Lee remaining a major part of the team. Still, he understood. Lee was a Korean American who longed to elevate the flavorful food he loved to a fine-dining clientele.

Shane dunked his head under the water and then popped back up.

"That's not all." With the setting sun casting a shadow over Reg's face, Shane could see the disquiet in his brother's eyes.

"Okay, what?" Shane didn't want to hear whatever it was Reg was going to say, but knew he needed to.

"Rick reviewed the monthlies in New York and there are big discrepancies in the cash receipts." Rick was their accountant in charge of balancing their books.

"Meaning what?"

"Meaning someone at the restaurant is stealing from us."

Not again. This had happened before. Unfortunately, when cash changed hands sometimes some of it disappeared. But it had never been a large enough amount to warrant the tightness currently in Reg's voice.

"How much money?"

Reg gave Shane a figure that set his pulse racing.

He pushed away from the side of the pool. This was everything he disliked about being in business. Dealing with staff and money and logistics was never his forte. All he'd ever wanted was just to cook and let his brother handle the rest of it. Yet now it was do or die. If Murphy Brothers Restaurants was going to have a future, he was going to have to extend himself past that comfort zone and start tackling these problems head-on.

Yet he wasn't sure he'd be able to. Knew that he, himself, was the biggest problem.

Shane dove deep underwater and swam the length of pool without coming up for air. Took a quick gulp at the other end and then did the same on the way back. When he emerged, Reg hadn't moved and was staring out at nothing in particular.

"Race." Shane challenged his brother to a lap across the pool. A slight grin crossed Reg's thin lips. Growing up, neither Murphy brother was a star athlete. Reg was more likely to have a book in his hand than a ball. But Shane would walk over to the playground in their Brooklyn neighborhood and shoot some basketball with whatever kids were hanging around.

"Go." The two brothers sprinted through the water. Shane narrowly edged Reg to the end of the pool. He felt nothing at his victory. It was just a stall tactic before continuing the conversation.

The problem was they were both spending so much time in Vegas. They'd been flying back and forth to the other restaurants as much as possible, but that was no substitute for being there night after night.

When they opened the Los Angeles restaurant, they had taken turns being on each coast. And opening the Las Vegas location had been manageable because they had thought the New York restaurant was in capable hands. They were wrong.

"What are we going to do?" Shane looked straight at his brother.

"I don't think we have a choice. I'll have to go back to New York and be there every night to oversee operations."

"Reg, you know I can't run things on my own here."

No one knew better than Reg that, not only was Shane incapable of the minutia involved in operating the restaurants, but since Melina died his concentration and patience were at zero. Even the cookbook, which should have been a joy, eluded him.

"We've got Rachel in LA training Enrique to be general manager here." Reg was focusing on solutions, thank goodness. "We'll bring him to Vegas now and Rachel can talk him through whatever comes up."

Shane would feel better with Enrique here. Many of the new staff had been hired. Perhaps some could start earlier than agreed upon to provide extra help.

"I'll be back a few days before the opening," Reg continued. "We'll still talk every day."

Shane's brother was a smart man who could have had a career doing anything he wanted. The two grew up working in the Brooklyn diner that their grandmother started, and then in the Lolly's chain named after her.

Their predispositions started early. Shane

was always at Grandma Lolly's apron, learning to cook the sturdy Irish dishes that she had learned from her own mother who'd brought them with her when she emigrated from Limerick. And young Reg kept his eye on the money, suggesting that they add a particular menu item or buy from certain vendors in order to maximize profit. When Shane proved to be a true culinary prodigy, Reg saw the business opportunity. They had a symmetry that had worked.

For a few years. Until Melina died. Until new chefs started grabbing the public's attention. Until the already reclusive Shane disappeared into himself.

"There's more," Reg continued.

Shane splashed water on his face and exhaled an extended breath through his nose. He didn't know how much more he could take in one night. "Okay, better to have it all dumped at once."

"It's about Brittany."

"Our assistant bar manager in New York?"

"Yes."

"What?"

* * *

Audrey fought with the zipper of the flowered dress she'd had on for the engagement shoot earlier. She hadn't been thrilled with it but they'd needed to take some practice publicity photos today. Without a minute to come back to change, she'd kept the dress on all day but now tugged it off and threw it across the room, narrowly missing Shane's face on the stand-up photo that was still propped in her bungalow. She had to rush to an appointment to pick a wedding gown. With only a month until the ceremony, there was barely time to have it ordered and altered.

Charging around the room in her white undies, she no longer cared what cardboard Shane thought of her. In her secret nightstand drawer, she reached for one of the stashed chocolates she had brought from Philadelphia. Which, although it was her absolute favorite kind, paled in comparison to the caramel cake Shane had teased her with a little while ago.

Her eyes rolled back in her head at the memory of that warm and gooey concoction delighting her taste buds. And how he had fed it to her with his fingers. His fingers! His thick, insistent fingers. She should have been deeply offended by his informality. Yet instead she'd been so powerfully aroused she could hardly keep her eyes open.

Once again, she thanked her lucky stars that she was marrying this man's brother and not him. Around Shane, who could even concentrate on anything?

As she chewed the familiar nougat robed in the fine chocolate of her Philadelphia candy, she couldn't remember a day in months when she hadn't craved and then savored this exact flavor. Yet suddenly, there was something unsatisfying about it. It tasted fine. But ordinary. Not the embodiment of heaven on earth she'd once thought it was.

Not able to name what, she hankered for something different. For something she'd be surprised to know she wanted. She glowered at Shane's photo and indicted him, "You did this! It's your fault! With your *pan de dulce de leche* on your warm fingers. Leave me be!"

After buttoning up a cotton shirt and slipping on jeans, she walked out her door and over to the hotel's half-built spa and salon. There, the manager Natasha had set up a temporary dressing room for her. Audrey had also called on Jesse, one of their stylists, to select some sample dresses. He wheeled them in on a rack.

"These will be far too long on you but we just want to get the idea, yeah?" Jesse said as he lifted one of the gowns and hung it on a hook for Audrey to try.

She inspected the dress.

Wedding gowns. She was here to choose a wedding gown. There had never been a clear picture in her mind of the actual ceremony binding her to Reg. If it wasn't for their new concept of using the wedding for hotel publicity, she might have married him in a courthouse. A simple legal transaction. Perhaps she'd have worn a plain white business suit.

Now that her nuptials were going to be photographed for the public's enticement, a full-on fantasy wedding was called for. Was the dress in front of her *the one*, as a bride who'd thought about it for years and poured over magazines and websites might know? Audrey didn't have the slightest idea. But it was worth a try.

Jesse zipped her into the mermaid-style dress with its slim line from the bosom to the knee where it then flared out down to the floor. Audrey examined herself in the three-sided mirror he had carried in.

The look was only okay. With her own curves above and below her waist, the extra slant outward at the bottom of the dress seemed out of proportion. Too zigzaggy.

Standing behind her in the mirror, Jesse gave a hoist up from under the arms and then a tug at the knee. After thorough consideration from every angle he concluded, "Not our dress."

The next one he helped her into was a tea-length lacy dress with sleeves and a very full skirt. The under layers crunched with every move she made. Once she saw herself in the mirror, it was an easy vote. She was completely lost in all the volume. It even made her head look disproportionately large.

"All gussied up in big-girl clothes, yeah?" Jesse joked, in complete compliance with the veto.

After that came a cream-colored gown that fit her like a glove. It was a strapless silk shantung number with plenty of structure meant to hold all of a busty girl's parts in place. It cinched at the waist with a band of fabric, then hugged her round hips and fell straight to the floor. A thigh-high slit would allow for movement while dancing.

In keeping with that swinging early 1960s Vegas look the hotel evoked, the dress could have been worn by any of the va-va-voom movie stars of that era. Although Audrey guessed those great ladies had a little more height than she did at her shrimpy five-foot-two.

Still, she felt gorgeous in it.

"Now *that* is your dress." Jesse knew it, too.

"Aw," Natasha called over from the shelves where she was stocking salon products.

Jesse fluffed out Audrey's hair to give it some bounce. And a pair of pumps he brought perfectly matched the gown. Audrey couldn't take her eyes off her reflection in the mirror. Her heart banged against her chest, as if it was fighting to break out.

She'd helped when needed with weddings at the hotels, knew a little about everything from invitations to ring pillows to emergency shoe repair.

But now that it had finally come to her own? Would Audrey wear this spectacular dress to consecrate a marriage in which she'd never have to risk putting love and trust to the test?

That was what she wanted. Wasn't it?

"Shane showed me his heap of half-baked notes," she told her dad in his office before the Murphys arrived. She'd come over after the dress fitting. The brothers had asked for an evening meeting.

"Pun intended." Daniel couldn't resist, but quickly turned serious. "We need all of these pieces to come together."

Everything was riding on this hotel. They had sunk a lot more money than they had intended to into its overhaul. The Girards were in debt.

"We'll be on top again," Daniel said softly.

"I let you down." Audrey chewed her lower lip. "Three years ago when I was at the helm, a lot of things started to go wrong for us."

"No. I'm so proud of how much you handled. It was me. I neglected my personal relationships with some our investors. We lost good staff at the other properties because I wasn't on top of their needs. Then we got a later start on this project than we should have. It all added up."

The time leading up to Jill's death would always be a thorn in both Daniel and Audrey's sides. When his wife got sick, Daniel became unable to concentrate. He let deadlines pass on important decisions and abandoned the constant follow-up that kept the hotels at the high benchmarks Girard was known for.

Audrey had clearly seen what was happening and jumped in. She temporarily stepped into his shoes, even operating from his corner office at the Philadelphia headquarters. Knowing enough about each department to provide a stopgap, she kept the company afloat.

Running the company provided her a perfect excuse to distance herself from her dying mother, who had made it clear that she didn't want Audrey around. "I don't want you to see me like this," Jill had told Audrey during one of their few visits. That was ironic given that her mother had never let Audrey truly *see* her. Jill had spent most of her life in the top floor of their townhouse in Philadelphia's exclusive Rittenhouse Square, hiding behind a veil of alcohol and pills.

Daniel saw his wife in a different light. He had loved her so completely he always held on to the belief that he could *fix* her. As if she were one of the faded grand hotels they were able to revamp with enough care and repair. He never comprehended how unwanted Jill had made Audrey feel. But Audrey would always know. She'd carry it with her for the rest of her life. It had shaped her into the person she was. A person who wasn't going to love or expect to be loved by anyone.

Therefore, during those grueling months of Jill's demise, Daniel chose one path and Audrey chose another. Once Jill died, Daniel wallowed in grief for a few months, and then his enthusiasm for the hotels gradually returned.

"Regrets?" she asked her dad.

"Of course not." He nodded. "You?"

"A sky full."

She'd said the same thing to Shane last night when they shared a heart-to-heart talk that lasted into the wee hours. Granted, it was with cardboard Shane. But he really seemed to understand her.

The brothers arrived. Reg told them about the turmoil in New York and his decision to leave the next day.

Then he confessed his feelings about his assistant bar manager, Brittany. "I'm in love with her. I am so sorry, Audrey."

What? Who was Brittany? He was calling the marriage off?

Blood palpitated through every vein in Audrey's body. She had just picked out a wedding gown! Worked day and night to tie up loose ends in Philadelphia so that she could shift her operations to Las Vegas in time to not only open the hotel but to plan a lavish wedding! And he was in love with someone else?

"I flew out here with an open mind to seeing the plan through with you." Reg rubbed his palms back and forth. "But I can't go through with it. It wouldn't be fair to either of us. I seem to have only just realized that I was missing something important in my life. Something I want to make room for."

"Lo-ove. You want love. You fell in love."

Stunned, Audrey repeated herself like a babbling idiot.

Shane shifted in his armchair without taking his eyes off Audrey. He'd obviously already known what Reg had come to say. It was so humiliating to have Shane in the room while this bombshell was being dropped on her! She directed a piercing stare right back at him.

Once she wrapped her mind around it, the news provoked a confusing mix of emotions in her. Rejection. More rejection for her to endure. But also liberation. In reality, Reg had been off-kilter since he'd arrived, and Audrey had sensed that something was amiss. Their fathers had agreed on this match a long time ago but she didn't know Reg all that well. She'd assumed they were kindred spirits in their desire for pragmatic companionship and nothing more.

Perhaps he was committed to fulfilling his family duty. But had secretly longed for love and for children all along. He was entitled to that, which he surely wasn't going to find with her. Ever.

She wouldn't want to be responsible for holding him back from what he wanted.

Audrey could no longer deny that the agreement had been like a safety net that she had been relying on. In the back of her mind she'd had a long-standing engagement to a pleasant man and she hadn't had to give her personal life any further thought. Her heart belonged to the hotels. Audrey had it in her plans for so long that she was going to end up with Reg, she hardly knew who she would be without this pact.

Yet, returning Shane's penetrating stare, she was suddenly, oddly, keen to find out.

Maybe Vegas was where she would discover herself. After all, she was out here in the boundless new frontier, in the Wild West.

Daniel uttered the same words to Reg as she would have. "I wish you every happiness. We can't wait to meet Brittany." After all, she no longer had claims to him.

"Thank you, sir. I'll bring her back with me for the opening."

"Forgive me for sounding callous—" Daniel looked to Reg and then to Shane "—but the plans we had for the hoopla and engagement events to open the property were critical to bringing in bookings. That leaves a big hole in our promotional campaigns. I know you need a strong launch as much as we do."

Shane remained silent, elbows on the arms of the chair and his legs spread wide apart. Still looking at Audrey. She felt naked under his gaze, having to remind herself that it was only his photo and not he who had seen her flitting around her bungalow in her undies earlier. His attention was unrelenting. Was he pitying her now that she'd essentially been jilted at the altar?

And now everyone was on to the next piece of business? She couldn't catch up.

"What about a substitute fiancé?" Reg suggested.

"Hmm..." Daniel weighed the idea. "Even though it wouldn't tie the hotel to the restaurant, it would still generate buzz about the property and we could show off how much we have to offer for special occasions."

"Then you can just break the engagement off after a year or so when it has faded in the public's memory."

"Who then? Befitting hotel royalty, it would

be ideal if it was someone in the industry." Daniel rubbed his chin as if massaging a pretend beard.

Reg rubbed his own chin the same way. "What about Dean Ryder, the catering manager at the Bellagio? He's single."

"I think he's gay," Daniel answered.

"Does that matter in this setup?" Reg asked.

"Brian Haywood, maître d' at Scallops is single," Daniel suggested.

"But, then again, would it behoove us to partner with someone from another hotel?" Reg questioned.

"It should be someone in house," Daniel agreed.

"I'm right here, folks!" Audrey finally erupted. "Don't talk about me like I'm not in the room!" First her arranged marriage was called off and then, within minutes, they were talking about a replacement.

Shane let out a huge belly laugh, the first sound out of him.

He winked at Audrey. Then rested his hand on the inside of his thigh.

The sight of which halted her breathing and caused her lower jaw to drop open.

Just as Daniel and Reg both froze and stared at Shane.

"What about…?" Daniel mused.

"Nah," Reg rejected the thought.

"Think about it," Daniel insisted.

"It might work…" Reg slowly nodded at the possibility.

"You couldn't ask for a spicier publicity match-up," Daniel pressed.

"The beautiful hotelier and the sexy chef," Reg continued.

"No way!" Shane and Audrey both shouted in unison when they realized what the other two were devising.

Even if it was just for publicity, she couldn't pose alongside Shane Murphy as the happy couple. He was far too moody and complicated. She couldn't possibly handle the way he made her feel. He made her *feel*. Always had.

Reg didn't make her *feel* anything. Audrey wasn't ever going to take a chance again on feeling. She'd let herself go from a hurt child to a wounded adult. Any more pain and she might not be able to get out of bed in the morning. The "no feel" principle was her trump card.

Finally Shane leaned forward in his chair and spoke up. "Absolutely not. I don't have the time to get into shenanigans surrounding a phony engagement." He was clearly as against the idea as she was, thank goodness. "Look, we're going to have to turn the cookbook project into our prime strategy. That's going to be the focal point of the campaigns. My first book. International distribution. Promoted with TV tapings at the new restaurant and all over the property. Hotel Girard Las Vegas as the place to be!"

They were all surprised to hear Shane talk about things from such a businessman's point of view.

"Let's be honest," Reg said, "The editor quit. You fired our public relations coordinator as well as your literary agent. You've been struggling with the book all along."

Shane exchanged a heartfelt unspoken moment with his brother. "Well I'm going to have to change my tune, aren't I?"

"Thank you," Reg said softly, obviously knowing how hard this was likely to be for Shane.

"I'm here to help," Audrey chimed in.

"You're going to do more than help, Sugar." Shane pointed his finger at her. "Clearly, I can't direct and manage this by myself. We're doing this together. As a matter of fact, you're in charge!"

CHAPTER FOUR

INTRODUCING MR. AND MRS. Shane Murphy. Yes, Audrey and Shane Murphy will attend. Hello, have you met my husband, Shane Murphy?

Whaaaaat?

The following day, Audrey couldn't stop playing images in her head as she skirted from meeting to meeting. What if she had agreed to a fake marriage with Shane?

The toasts of Las Vegas, the Murphys returning to town and descending the steps of their private jet after a quick weekend in Geneva where Shane received an award for restaurant excellence. The Murphys partying the night away at Vegas's newest exclusive club, Shane graciously allowing handsome movie stars to salsa dance with his wife. The Murphys sailing around the Greek Islands on their second wedding anniversary. Is Mrs. Murphy sporting a baby bump above the teeny triangle of designer bikini she wears?

That's publicity and public relations for you. Even Audrey's fantasy mind knew how to put a spin on everything.

The reality wasn't as pretty. First, her riskless and sane arranged engagement had fallen apart. Second, she was set to work closely with a man who made the ground she stood on shaky every time she was near him.

Shane ignited her, gave her a sense of something spontaneous and out of her control. She worried he could blow her "no feel" policy to smithereens.

But they were both professionals and this was critical business. All she had to do was get him through the cookbook and publicity needed for a successful opening. Then she could back away from him. Easy peasy.

The evening was spent in her bungalow toiling on her laptop, finishing up work on the summer events she had planned at Hotel Girard Cape Cod. Looking at photos of the Atlantic Ocean shoreline gave her a bit of a shiver, replaying again that brush with Shane ten years ago in the Caribbean Sea at St. Thomas.

It was almost midnight when she powered down her computer. Her dad knew that Audrey liked to swim and had mentioned that the employee pool was in operation. It was late, but the idea sounded too refreshing to pass up. Quickly changing into her bathing suit, she stuck her tongue out at cardboard Shane as she left her bungalow.

The pool area was completely empty. No lights had been left on so Audrey treaded carefully. She put her towel down on a chair and removed her bathing suit cover-up and flip-flops. With a brave plunge, she dove straight into the deep end. The water felt divine as she sank into it, cool but not cold. In Philadelphia, she swam indoors, so it was a treat to be out under the bright moon. The midnight desert winds were strong and warm.

Swimming was an activity Audrey did as often as she could, both for exercise and as meditation. While her arms and legs rotated rhythmically through the water, lap after lap, one after the next, she could contemplate her day. Set goals for the next. And, occasionally, she could get a glimpse into the bigger pictures of life.

Each time she reached the edge of the pool, she turned and pushed off with both feet to start in the next direction. Back and forth. Back and forth.

Reg, she contemplated, was not the slightest bit attractive to her. That would have been good. Not sexy would rank as the number one quality she'd be looking for in a man if she ever did decide to wed. In the meantime, she'd have to steer clear of men like Shane, who stoked the fires she kept contained inside of her.

He was gorgeous. She spelled out each letter in time with an arm stroke as she swam. *G*, stroke, *o*, stroke, *r*, stroke, *g-e-o-u-s*.

Although her laps were smooth, she seemed to be cutting a lot of water because she felt waves of vibration moving across the pool.

She could see one day getting married to a man who could accept her limitations. No love. No trust. No need. She'd been down that road. Just because it was with her mother and not a romance didn't change the blackness in her heart. Anything more was out of the question.

Her past had shaped her into the person she was now, and her future was determined. Audrey wasn't going to care for someone or expect to be cared for in return. If a man even hinted at wanting that, he'd be off the list immediately.

It had seemed like it was going to be so easy with Reg. Darn.

As she swam, she thought about a time a decade earlier in St. Thomas. It had been the summer before she started college. Celebrity chef Shane, only twenty-four then and not yet married, had been contracted to cook a special seasonal menu in the dining room for two weeks while the Murphys were opening their Lolly's outlet. There had been huge hype for his appearance. The hotel was at capacity, the kitchen bustling with activity and food deliveries.

Shane was not only a hotshot, he was a hothead. She'd never heard a voice so loud it could rattle stacks of dishes in the kitchen. A boom that overpowered the clamor of pots and pans, of chopping and frying and grilling. Eighteen-year-old Audrey had somewhat understood that he was volatile because he was a perfectionist, uncompromising, expecting excellence in himself and others.

At the time, though, to her Shane was downright daunting. Scary, yet utterly thrilling in the way he'd hulk into the kitchen and throw down his motorcycle helmet and leather jacket. How he refused to don the Hotel Girard chef's coat, instead wearing T-shirts bearing the names of heavy-metal rock bands. His impossibly broad shoulders leading the eyes to a solid wall of chest and muscular arms. He was raw manpower, something young Audrey had never been exposed to so nakedly.

She pushed off into another lap in the pool. For a minute she thought she heard splashing, but she didn't see anything around her.

In St. Thomas, Reg had always been there somewhere in the background, holding up a file for his brother to review or soothing egos after one of Shane's outbursts. Wiry and calculating, Reg could slip in or out of a room without anyone noticing. Whereas Shane was a tidal wave whose undertow was always felt both before his arrival and after his departure. Shane had stolen all the air in her lungs every time she was near him.

Audrey felt a whoosh of water so strong it almost veered her off her straight lap. Maybe the pump system in the pool needed to be adjusted.

Then there had been that last night on the island. After the resounding success of those two weeks, the Murphy brothers were packing up to jet back to New York. The summer was ending and Audrey would be heading to college later that week.

As she often liked to do at night, she'd walked barefoot in the soft island sand down to the beach. The sky was dark blue as she waded into the sparkling water and then launched herself into a swim. Her young brain was swimming, as well, with mental images of that powerful dark chef who she wondered when she'd see again given their families' business dealings.

While she was swimming farther into the sea, she felt something slide up along her leg. At first she was frightened that it might be a shark, or another marine predator. But a human head poked out from under the water. She'd have recognized him anywhere, even in the darkness.

Those long crazy locks of hair were a wet and wild tangle framing his unshaven face. His lips glistened with moisture. Shane had come out for a swim, as well.

"Well, what do we have here?" he called to her with surprise, their heads bobbing above the water and the sound of the waves making it difficult to hear. "Why it's little Audrey Girard."

She'd felt so light-headed, she thought she might drown. The way he had slithered up beside her. Unintentionally, of course, but nonetheless he'd shocked her half to death. And then when she found it was him, a screaming awakening coursed through her. The mixture of attraction, fascination and fear was like nothing she'd ever felt before.

Or since.

No words had come out of her mouth. All she could do was summon all of her might to paddle herself back to shore as quickly as possible and run away in the sand.

A split second in the Caribbean Sea. A moment that she was never able to forget.

Why it's little Audrey Girard.

"We meet underwater again," came a low voice from the other side of the pool.

Audrey thought she might be hallucinating. Shane's words from a decade ago had just been looping over and over again in her head.

"What?" she stuttered into the Vegas night, blinking her eyes to try to focus.

He plied a few strokes and was quickly by her side. Shane. A decade later. "You discovered the pool. That you kindly built for the staff."

Get out of the water immediately, Audrey's mind directed. Yes, their fates were inexorably linked now in commercial partnerships. Yes, she'd be at his side working on the cookbook tomorrow. But there was no reason why she should be with him in a swimming pool at midnight.

"I'm glad you're making use of it," she stammered, her chest knocking so loud she thought she could hear it.

"Some turn of events, huh? I only just found out myself about Reg's change of heart."

"Yes." Move away from him. Audrey wasn't exactly sure what she was scared of, but terrified she was. Did she think that now because she was no longer engaged to Shane's brother, he might touch her? Or worse still, that she wouldn't be able to resist touching him? Many years may have passed but her gravitational pull toward Shane Murphy was as strong as ever. And, just like last time in the water, escape seemed the only option.

"I'm going to get some sleep." She had to get away from him. Tomorrow was another day. Best to take them one at a time. "I'll meet you at your kitchen. At noon."

Audrey hoisted herself out of the pool using the stepladder in the deep end. Which was nowhere near her towel. Just as she knew he would, Shane stayed in the water and watched her in what was enough moonlight for him to get a full outline of her body. Thankfully, she wasn't wearing a bikini. But, still, the athletic one-piece bathing suit didn't leave anything to the imagination.

As she crossed the length of the pool toward her things, he used both hands to rake back his long wet hair. "Sugar—" he smiled up from the shimmering water "—you sure grew up."

* * *

A glistening flesh-and-blood Shane in the moonlit water an hour ago. Ten-year-old memories of Shane in the Caribbean Sea. Now she was back to cardboard Shane in her bungalow. Everywhere Audrey turned, she found him.

After a hot shower, Audrey was still flustered by the interaction at the pool. He'd really gotten under her skin. All of a sudden she was no longer attached to the man she was to marry, yet it was his brother she couldn't stop thinking about.

Tossing and turning in bed, she was wide-awake and aware. Giving up on sleep, she switched on the lamps, propped herself up in bed and opened her laptop.

She'd promoted a date for the press to tour the hotel, but she needed to get to the nuts and bolts of the event. After welcoming them at the rooftop pool, they'd be taken on a guided tour of the property. She'd have the spa staff treat them to mini massages and give them goody bags filled with samples of the hotel's signature body care products. Then they'd reconvene on the roof for a reception.

"What should we serve for a light brunch?" Audrey asked cardboard Shane as matter of factly as she might have if her dad had been in the room.

Weirder still, she received an answer. "Right, morning pastries and fruit kebobs would be easier than something they have to sit down to eat with a fork," she said aloud, typing in Shane's recommendation, knowing that she had gone insane.

"That would be great." She complimented Shane's idea of a station serving flavored coffees. "Okay, we'll do a dark chocolate, a hazelnut and an orange."

His suggestions for mini smoothies and for the buffet setup were all noted. "Thank you for your help."

When she couldn't keep her eyes open any longer, she ended the meeting by flicking off the light.

Shane's photo said, "Good night, Sugar."

The next day, Audrey arrived in the kitchen. She expected to find Shane at work on the cookbook recipes. The lights were on. Yet the kitchen was silent, save for the hum of the re-frigeration system.

"Shane?" she called out in case he was in one of the nooks or walk-in cabinets within the large space. "Shane?"

There was no reply.

Audrey had been in here with him yesterday when he unceremoniously dumped his pile of recipe ideas out onto his desk. And the day be-fore when he'd ushered her and Reg out. She'd yet to have a quiet moment to really take in the scale of the kitchen. It, like the dining room, was by far the largest at any of the Girard ho-tels.

Zones were designated for cleaning, cutting, frying, sautéing, baking, grilling, plating and so on. Boxes of state-of-the-art equipment, appli-ances and tools were marked for their station. There were food prep tables, dishwashing sta-tions, freezers, ice makers, storage areas. There appeared to be a place for everything. Based on what she'd seen of how Shane functioned, this level of organization seemed impossible.

She looked to the spot where Shane had popped that divine dulce de leche cake into her mouth. Sadly, the pan was no longer there. Who had eaten it, she wondered? With envy.

"What are you doing here?" Shane's voice stunned her as he charged in wearing a motorcycle helmet, each of his big hands lugging half a dozen grocery bags. He plopped them all onto a prep table.

"We had an appointment for noon. To work on the cookbook."

Shane peeled off his helmet and laid it on the counter. He finger-combed his long hair away from his face. Audrey wondered what it would be like to do that for him.

"You're right, we did."

"What would be a good way to get started? Should we look at your idea file again?" Audrey asked, referring to that collection of notes scrawled on napkins and pieces of cardboard. If that was all Shane had to go from, it would have to do.

"Those are just scribbles. I haven't given them much thought."

"Well, did you jot them down because you were hoping they might be right for the cookbook? Didn't you work with an editor on it already?"

"He was a moron," Shane shot back. He dug into the grocery bags he had tossed onto the counter.

"But did you…"

"Let's make a ceviche," he interrupted. "I got some lovely red snapper filets I want to play around with."

He quickly washed his hands, unwrapped the fish from its paper and laid it on a cutting board. With a knife selected from a drawer, he swiftly sliced the fish into bite-sized chunks. They were dispatched into a bowl.

Reaching in another bag for limes, he halved and squeezed the juice of five of them over the fish. He reached for a disposable glove to mix in the lime with his fingers. Then he placed the bowl in a refrigerated drawer.

"Is this for the cookbook?"

"Sugar, I don't know at this point. This is how I work. Let's just try some things."

"Stop calling me Sugar."

The used glove was tossed in the trash, and

the cutting board and knife deposited into a sink.

Next, he pulled out a clean cutting board and knife. Swung around to locate the tomatoes in his grocery bags, and rinsed them under a sink. With breakneck speed and precision, they were diced.

He opened another drawer for a clean spoon to scoop up a pile of the ruby-red tomatoes and feed them to Audrey.

They were surely the juiciest, most flavorful she'd ever tasted.

"Beautiful, right?"

Audrey knew he was talking about food. There was no rationale for the jealousy she felt when he called the tomatoes beautiful and the red snapper lovely. Was she competing with a fish? And why would she care anyway?

"Get me the jalapeño peppers. They're in a plastic bag," he directed her. What was she now, his kitchen assistant? She supposed she could be, and should be, if that would help get the cookbook done.

But Shane's style was hard to take. He was too quick. Too forceful. Too impulsive. Too right up in her face. Feeding her yesterday with his fingers and today with a spoon. For heaven's sake!

Yet all of that spontaneity jostled her to the core. He was hypnotizing. Making her want to be part of whatever he was doing.

When she handed him the jalapeños their fingers touched, and flickers flew up her arm.

"If you ever work with these, be careful not to touch your eyes until your hands are clean," he cautioned about the peppers. Because their heat might burn her, just as Shane was doing with his very being?

He chopped the peppers into tiny minces.

"Are we keeping a measurement?" she reminded herself of the task at hand. "In order duplicate the recipe?"

"We don't know if we have a recipe yet."

"But if we change it later, at least we'll know where we started from."

Shane's nostrils flared. As if in slow motion, his jaw tensed and then twitched. He shot her a scowl so scornful it made her take a step backward. Her mere suggestion of a method to accomplish one recipe for the cookbook upset him.

"I think I know what I'm doing in my own kitchen."

Yet she could tell from the lost look in his eyes that his reaction was a heartbreaking combination of pain and frustration. Half of her wanted to run away while the other half wished she could hug him.

She cast her eyes downward for a momentary respite.

Shane put his knife down and busied himself at another station unpacking a box. Leaving Audrey standing with a lump in her throat.

What kind of monster had he become? Shane asked himself the question as he arranged and rearranged jars of spices he had ordered. He wished he hadn't quit smoking years ago because a lungful of tar was just what he was really craving right now.

Yes, he did want this new Shane's Table restaurant to bring him back to the short list of best chefs in the world. Yes, he did know that an internationally distributed cookbook and TV special would put his name back in the limelight.

Yes, he did understand that this was do or die for the Murphy Brothers Restaurants company.

Then why was he being such an ass?

He looked over to Audrey as if she held the answer.

Down inside, he knew.

A man doesn't just snap back from a wrong marriage that ends in his wife's death. An awful death that he might have been able to prevent had he taken action. He would always blame himself. He still wanted to scream, to cry, to shout his truth. That he felt responsible for Melina's death and perhaps he always would. That he should wear a sign around his neck that read Don't Get Close. That he was never to be trusted. He tried to issue Audrey a silent warning.

Two years had passed since Melina's death and Shane hadn't shaken off any of it. He'd sat wordlessly through appointments with grief counselors. Taken a soul-searching trip to Europe. Spent lots of time with his parents. Gotten back to swimming every day. None of it had helped. Setting up the Las Vegas location for the Feed U Project, the charitable organization his family oversaw, was one positive thing he had accomplished. There was purpose in working with kids who might otherwise fall victim to poor nutrition.

But he surely didn't have a clear plan for the future of his restaurants, nor the energy and enthusiasm he'd need to see it come to fruition. He'd run on Reg's fumes. Nothing was ever going to move forward unless he created some steam of his own.

For starters, he wished he could undo having just gotten annoyed with Audrey.

He finished inventorying the jars just as a delivery of equipment arrived. Shane shook the driver's hand and instructed him where to place the order.

Audrey was still standing exactly where he had left her a few minutes ago, though she was on her phone. Her time was valuable. She was here to work. How could he explain to her that it was a calling beyond his own will that had steered him to create the original, innovative dishes that made him a success? And that he didn't know how to get his inspiration back.

Her blond hair looked like spun silk. He

guessed that her sensual body would be soft in his hands. Like he could take a trip to heaven by exploring every supple inch. He'd seen many inches indeed by the pool last night. His center had wrung with an ache he didn't know he could feel anymore.

Great, the only woman in years to remind him that he still had a pulse was completely off-limits! He might be ready now to satisfy carnal desires with a female, but it certainly wouldn't be with a corporate partner he'd known for years and would be working with for many to come. Who was supposed to have become his sister-in-law! That was all kinds of wrong.

If Shane was ready, perhaps he could start thinking about dating again. But nothing ongoing, of course. He'd never be in a long-term relationship again. Not after what he'd done, or failed to do, with Melina. It had cost them the highest price imaginable. He'd lost the right to a relationship where he would be counted on.

He had always figured that's why his dad and Daniel's royal match up for Reg and Audrey had taken shape in the first place. After Shane's catastrophe of a marriage, the dads got spooked and decided to step in. He could hardly blame them.

So it's Brittany in New York, huh, Reg? She was a former drug addict who had been clean and sober for years and was a hard-working employee they valued. Shane was happy for his brother. Why shouldn't Reg fall in love if that's what he wanted? His brother had only dated a few women, but never for longer than a few months because he'd always been so preoccupied with the business. What a stable, serious man his brother was. It was touching to see the light in Reg's eyes as he spoke of Brittany and this unexpected turn of events. If for no other reason but for Reg's sake, Shane had to pull himself together to accomplish what he'd told his brother he would here in Vegas.

He couldn't gauge whether Audrey was devastated or relieved that her wedding was called off. In any case, he wished he hadn't been such a jerk a few minutes ago.

After the deliveryman unloaded the order in the kitchen, Audrey and Shane faced each other at an impasse.

"What's going to get you motivated again?" she asked in earnest.

"I don't know." Shane had an impulse and grabbed Audrey by the hand. "Let's go."

"Go where?" she protested. "We need to work."

He snatched up his keys and helmet, and tugged her toward the door. "Come on. I can at least show you something that's become important to me."

Outside, he freed the spare helmet he had locked in his motorcycle. He couldn't remember the last time he'd had a rider with him. And had to admit to himself that he was turned on by the idea of Audrey's arms around his waist and her breasts pressing into his back while they zoomed along city streets.

"Oh, no. No. I can't." Audrey shook her head as Shane tried to hand her the helmet. She fumbled for words. "I mean, look at what I'm wearing."

She gestured to her black business dress and heels. True, not appropriate for a ride on a motorbike.

"Why don't you run over to your bungalow and change clothes?" he suggested.

She shook her head even more adamantly. "No."

"Why not?"

"Because I'm afraid. Okay? Are you happy now? You got me to admit it. I don't want to ride on your motorcycle."

Her honesty pulled at his heart. His lips gravitated forward, compelled to kiss her.

Almost.

Thankfully, he pulled back in time.

"Alright, Sugar." He twisted his nose and locked both helmets onto the bike. "We'll take the Jeep."

She let out a whoosh of relief, making him realize how scared she had been. "Where are we going?"

CHAPTER FIVE

EVEN THOUGH SHE wouldn't get on his motorcycle, Shane liked having Audrey next to him
in his Jeep while he drove away from the Strip.
In the months he'd been in Vegas, he couldn't
think of a time he'd had anyone besides his
brother in the vehicle with him.

With the roof retracted, they motored in the
open air. Audrey's hair bounced every ray of
sunlight as it whooshed around her face, and
her dark sunglasses gave her a fashion that har-
kened back to movie stars of yesteryear. As they
passed the intersection where he'd make a turn
if he was going to his apartment, it tortured
him to imagine the multiple activities he'd like
to engage in with her if they were going there.

Instead, he continued on toward their destination. It never ceased to amaze him that just a
few blocks away from the Strip, away from the
lights and the jumbotrons, the endless proces-

sion of people and the clanking of the casinos, Las Vegas was an actual city. The streets were lined with gas stations, fast food restaurants, medical offices and shopping centers. Residents had jobs and kids. There was suburban wealth and the slums of poverty. Most tourists never saw any of it. The whole point of their visit was the total escape from real life that the Strip offered.

When he pulled into the parking lot of the nondescript industrial building, Audrey gave him a questioning look.

He sprang out of the Jeep and went around to the other side to open her door and lead her to the entrance. With a turn of his key, the metal door in the front of the building unlatched and he pushed it open.

The cavernous space was set up as one enormous kitchen, equipped with many work stations in stainless steel. The walls were redbrick and unfussy lighting hung from the ceiling.

"What is this?" Audrey asked.

"We teach kids to cook here," Shane said as he pointed to the plastic banner that hung from a wall-to-wall shelf. It read Welcome to Feed U.

"Feed U," Audrey repeated. "Is this what you do in your spare time?"

"I set this one up a few months ago," Shane explained, "My family is overseeing about a dozen of these kitchens. You know, a lot of kids are at risk of malnutrition. Maybe they don't have a parent around during the day to supervise their eating. Or parents are passing on bad habits to their kids. We try to help as many as we can learn about healthy eating."

At the far end of the space, sun-weathered Lois sat working at her desk. "Hey, Shane," she called.

"Hi, Lois," he returned, and then told Audrey, "she's our kitchen manager. Don't mess with Miss Lois."

"I heard that," Lois yelled over.

"My man," teenage Santiago called as he came through the side door with a half dozen six-year-olds in tow. Each kid held a herb or vegetable in their hand.

"Ah, you've been out to the garden," Shane said to them.

No matter what was going on in his life, as soon as Shane was with the kids he started to relax. The pressure was off. He didn't have to be a big, fancy chef. In a way, Feed U had nothing at all to do with his distinguished career or running the restaurants. But because his family lent their famous name to it, the Feed U Project was growing. Plans for even more locations worldwide were in the works.

Santiago and Shane did their four-part handshake. Shane high-fived each of the kids.

"I want you all to meet my friend Audrey," Shane said. "Santiago here is our teen supervisor."

Audrey fumbled trying to follow Santiago's handshake. She raised her palm toward the kids in a tentative hello.

"What's everybody cooking today?" Shane asked.

"Salad with matos," one of the kids answered.

"Tomatoes," Shane corrected. "Cool."

"And kooky-umbers," another kid added.

"Yeah, cucumbers." Shane nodded. "What else are you making?"

"We're baking bread," piped up a living doll with curly blond hair.

Although he was sure he'd never have kids,

couldn't be trusted with that kind of responsi-
bility, he loved working with them. There was
never anything fake with children. Everything
was alive. Nothing else existed except the honesty of the moment. That little cutie who'd just
announced they were baking bread was recep-
tive and radiant with pure optimism.

Shane could vaguely remember how that felt.
A happy, if impatient, kid himself, his parents
and Grandma Lolly had paid attention to him.
They were able to see that his intuition in the
kitchen as a child was something unique. It was
their belief in him that had propelled Shane's
rise to such a high level at such a young age.

And he'd rewarded their faith and nurturance
by becoming a burned-out grouch. Who'd made
a rash marriage that had led to a horrifying
conclusion. All of which brought him to almost
burying himself alive.

Had he succeeded, or could he find his way
home from *almost*?

What had made him just smile wistfully at
Audrey?

"Okay." He summoned his attention back to

the kids. "What are the three rules we always have to remember in the kitchen?"

"Learn the safe way," the kids all chanted. Which was followed by "Always cook with an adult."

"That's right," Shane affirmed. "And what's the third important thing to remember?"

The kids shouted, "Rock 'n' roll!"

Audrey giggled.

With that, Shane flicked a switch on the wall and music played from several speakers scattered around the room. He wiggled his hips and the kids followed suit.

"You work with Santiago and help the kids knead the bread dough," Shane said to Audrey. "I'm going to cut the vegetables and then they can compose their salads."

"Oh, no. I'll just watch." Audrey seemed uncomfortable. In fact, she looked at the kids like the precious and fragile miracles they were.

"Why?" Shane probed.

"I'm, uh, I'm not used to being around children," she whispered.

"Here's your opportunity. They won't break."

"I wouldn't want to take any chances," she said with her chin pointed downward.

"Chances of what?"

"That I couldn't protect them."

Not a day went by that Shane didn't have a thought like that. He wondered where Audrey's fear of herself originated.

"I don't think there's much danger in kneading bread dough," he tried to reassure her. She was acting very out of character. Not the spunky and confident go-getter she was at the hotel. "Did your mom have you help in the kitchen when you were growing up?"

"No," she said quickly, "my mother wouldn't let me come in the kitchen. She said that it wasn't a place for children."

Those words stung Shane. The kitchen was for everyone. It was a place where love could be passed from generation to generation. Food could mean care. Or rejuvenation. Or bonding. He wished there had been someone to teach Audrey those lessons when she was a kid. No wonder she liked sweets. She found the pleasure of food that way. He'd have to work on her.

A life in restaurants had shown him a lot of

crazy eating habits that had nothing to do with food. Women so thin he could see their bones right through their skin who dined with powerful men yet never ate a morsel themselves. He'd learned that sometimes they didn't eat as a way of exercising control over food when they didn't have control in other areas of their lives.

Or those rich and important men who'd stuff so much food in their faces they'd become red and sweaty. Maybe they'd been criticized by their parents and now they were showing the world they deserved opulence because they had made something of their lives.

Shane had dozens of stories about the role of food in people's lives. That's why Feed U's mission was to help young people foster healthy relationships with eating.

"Come here, munchkin, what's your name?" He called the girl with the ringlets over.

"Mia."

"Mia, my friend Audrey here doesn't know anything about making bread. Can you help her?"

"It's easy," the little girl said. Then she lifted up her hand to take Audrey's and guided her to the work station. Audrey swallowed hard. Shane almost thought he saw her biting back tears. He fought an urge to go hold her, to wrap her in his arms and tell her everything was going to be okay no matter what it was she was carrying around in her soul. He wanted to right her wrongs. Release her from them.

But that wasn't his place. Nothing about their association with each other entitled him to really get to know her.

He couldn't help but visualize Audrey looking like little Mia when she was that age. The blond hair, the brown eyes, the determined set of their shoulders. Seeing them together pulled at Shane's heart. There was something unspeakably beautiful about how the young girl gave Audrey a ball of dough and showed her how to press it with the heels of her teeny hands.

Audrey glanced up and her eyes met Shane's. "I can see why this means a lot to you," she said to him. "It would have to me when I was a kid."

"Yeah, Shane's cool," Mia said.

"Yes. He is."

Shane scratched his beard stubble, humbled. Tonight he and Audrey were attending their

first strategic event. To show him off. She
wanted him seen in public, to become a glittering fixture on the Strip. Something he'd completed avoided, hovering in his kitchen day and
night.

They were going to a new nightclub at Caesars Palace. As his publicist, she'd escort him.
Soon they'd head back to the hotel to get ready.
It'd be an evening of limos, nice clothes, raz-
zle-dazzle.

Fine, Shane thought. He'd play the game, after
all, they were betting high to win. One thing he
knew was that, secretly, he was looking forward
to spending the evening with Audrey.

Just to keep her company, of course.

And it made good sense to at least get out of
the kitchen and be seen around Vegas. He'd
cut himself off from almost everyone except
his family. He had chef friends here. His old-
kitchen mates Tino and Loke were cooking on
the Strip, yet he hadn't seen them in all the
months he'd been coming into town to supervise
the construction of the restaurant. Worse still,
he hadn't gone out to see Josefina, the grandmo-
therly friend that he considered a mentor. He'd

talked to her on the phone but hadn't been able to face the look she'd give him, knowing in an instant how much of himself he'd let slip away.

He watched Santiago move around from kid to kid to be sure they were able to do the kneading. Shane liked the sixteen-year-old aspiring chef, who was earning high school service credits for helping the little ones. Santiago made his way over to Shane at the salad station.

"Shane, man, like, how do you create a recipe? Like, how do you know what ingredients to put together?"

A good question. One Shane had, apparently, forgotten how to answer. "I think one recipe kind of leads to the next," he managed. "You taste some dish you like. You figure out what's in it. That this tastes good with that. And then it occurs to you how you could make it better."

"Yeah but, like, how does that actually happen?"

Oh, if he only knew. Here he was opening up a high-profile restaurant in one of the top food destinations in the world, yet he couldn't find his way back to the imagination and originality that had brought him his initial acclaim. Where was the magic that his family had seen in him even as a young boy? Who had he become?

"Patience. Focus. Concentration." Shane tried to answer Santiago's question with what came to mind. His stomach wrenched into a knot, his fists balled involuntarily until his fingernails were digging into his flesh.

Why on earth couldn't he follow his own advice?

Audrey modeled in front of the mirror in her bungalow. She didn't like the fifth dress, either. Why she objected tonight to all of these dresses that she usually enjoyed wearing, she didn't know. The perfect one just wasn't jumping out.

Nix on the black fitted dress with the cap sleeves. Too somber.

With the many dressy occasions at the hotels, Audrey owned a substantial wardrobe. It was what the job demanded. Her dad, and her grandfather back when he was still alive, only had to choose from tuxedos and tailored suits when they represented the company at events. Men had it easy. Audrey owned clothes for black-tie affairs, celebrations, civic functions and sportswear, along with the conservative business dresses and skirts she wore most of the time.

No to the red dress with the ruffles down the front. Too froufrou.

When packing up in Philadelphia for her stay out here, she figured ball gowns were not going to be required and left those behind. Vegas nights would call for party frocks and cocktail dresses. She'd need to straddle the line between tasteful, the Girard brand promise, and current, so as to present herself as on top of trends. She'd packed a few suitcases full, along with shoes and accessories, knowing that someone at headquarters could send more of her things if she needed them.

The emerald green with the ruching at the waist? Better for a wedding guest.

It wasn't lack of selection that was prohibiting her from deciding on a dress for tonight. The truth was that she wanted to look good for Shane. Although she told herself that shouldn't matter one iota, it did. She was going out to a nightclub on the Las Vegas Strip with a devastatingly handsome and charismatic man. She hadn't done anything like that in…she couldn't even remember the last time. If an event she attended called for her to bring a *plus one*, it was always her dad. That duty was to have switched to Reg. Tonight it was Shane who needed the date.

Veto on the geometric pattern wrap dress. Too casual.

So while Audrey traveled the globe and certainly lived a life of culture and even luxury, for the moment she was a nervous teenager going out on a first date with her crush. "Whoosh," she said aloud. Better push those feelings out of the picture right now. They had no place in her world. This was not that kind of date.

Even though she had thought of Shane almost every day since she'd first laid eyes on him in St. Thomas ten years ago. How he skidded up to the entrance of the hotel on his motorcycle, yanked off his helmet and shook his hair out in the sea breeze. He'd spotted her, *little Audrey Girard*, that day in tennis whites holding her racquet as she crossed the valet station. He'd winked at her and she'd been mortified with embarrassment at his attention. Yet she'd never forgot it. Nor the chaos in the kitchen and especially not the late-night encounter in the sea.

That was then. This was business. It couldn't be anything more. She simply needed to put on clothes for the evening. The first dress she had tried on was the best. Copper-colored and satiny, it had a halter neck with a deep V in front and a slim bodice that gave way to a full skirt. The style was a bit retro 1950s, which suited her hourglass figure. The dress also had a modern edge with its length, which ended well above the knee, making her legs look longer than they really were. She paired it with metallic high-heeled sandals and an evening purse. Earlier, she'd begged Natasha at the salon to blow out her hair and do evening makeup on her face.

With her ensemble complete, she headed for the door. Giddiness and apprehension about seeing Shane competed within her despite her attempts to shut them down. Cardboard cutout Shane gave her an appreciated boost of confidence when he complimented her with "You look hot."

She blushed as she thanked him.

"You look hot," real Shane seconded with his seal of approval as he ushered her into the limo. He spiked her temperature, as well, in his slim-fitting black suit with a dress shirt and no tie. How did it happen that he chose a brown shirt that perfectly complemented the copper of her dress? Kismet. He slid in next to her, much closer than was necessary, before the chauffeur shut the car door.

Shane settled back against the leather seat. Whether he meant to or not, his trouser-clad leg brushed against her bare thigh. Acting on the urge to shift away would have been too obvious, so Audrey froze in place. Her skin tickled at the fresh smell of his wild hair, which brushed incongruously against the jacket of the fine suit he had on.

"Champagne?" Shane asked although he didn't wait for an answer as he expertly and cleanly popped the bottle's cork. He poured the bubbly into the two crystal flutes that had been set up for them. Caesars Palace wasn't far away from the Hotel Girard. Drinks weren't even in order, and Audrey never took more than a bit,

but it was a fun touch. And traffic moved no-
toriously slow on Las Vegas Boulevard.

"To our new venture." Audrey proposed a
toast. They clinked glasses and sipped.

Shane gave her a small smile. It wasn't one
of his sexy smirks. This one was intimate and
knowing, as if he saw right through to her soul.
Its focus tormented her.

"Why are you examining me like that?" she
asked after the silence stretched too long yet his
fix on her didn't waver.

"Wondering who you are," he rejoined quickly.
"We've been acquainted for a long time but I
don't really know a thing about you."

"I like movies and long walks on the beach,"
she kidded in a monotone about the typical get-
to-know-you answers.

"Me, too!" Shane played along.

"And cuddling with puppies."

"And world peace." Then he let the joking
subside. "I mean, I don't know anything *real*
about you."

"What do you want to know?"

"You strut around the hotel with your confer-
ences and your high-heeled shoes, yet today at

Feed U you looked like a scared little girl who couldn't find her mommy."

Her neck flushed. He was right. He'd seen her naked today. Not in a bathing suit at the pool under the moonlight where he might have been able to make out the shape of her body. No, she'd been exposed when she freaked out about being around the children and wasn't quick enough to cover up her emotional scars.

An only child, she didn't have nieces or nephews. Her work had her dashing from one of the Girard properties to the next, and their brand of boutique hotels tended to attract adults rather than families. She simply wasn't around kids very often and was uncomfortable in their presence. How odd, that as a twenty-eight-year-old woman she'd had almost no contact with children.

Part of her had wanted to go play in the garden with those kids today. To sing silly songs in the sunshine and cheer them on while they picked their "matos" and "kooky-umbers."

She'd almost come completely unglued when Shane asked if she'd ever cooked with her mother. Not only didn't Jill cook or let Audrey in the kitchen, but his question had brought back a particularly telling memory.

Audrey was not much older than the kids at Feed U when a girl at school had told her that her mother had baked her a birthday cake and that they had decorated it together. Already having a sweet tooth, that sounded like the most fun Audrey could imagine, to decorate a cake exactly how she wanted to. She mentioned it to Jill during her five-minute visit one night before bed.

When Audrey's birthday came around a couple of weeks later, Jill drove her to their hotel in Philadelphia. There, the pastry chef had laid out all of the necessary components for a birthday cake. Several flavors of cake to choose from, and icing with various colors to mix in, piping bags, candy sprinkles and sugar beads in every shape and variety.

But since Daniel was out of town and Jill had merely dropped Audrey off with the hotel's bell captain, it was with a kitchen assistant that the birthday girl decorated and ate her cake. A smile never once crossing her lips.

That was Jill in a nutshell. She'd adminis-

trated Audrey's upbringing rather than participating in it.

Being around the children at Feed U earlier
that day had made her wonder, and not for the
first time, what it would be like to have a child
herself. Yet that seemed impossible, unthink-
able. With the kind of lessons she'd learned
from Jill, she'd have no clue how to properly
parent and would no doubt fail miserably at it.
No way she'd let that happen!

Shane had pushed the wrong button and Audrey retaliated, knowing she was being defen-
sive but unable to bite her tongue. "I could say
the same about you. You skulk around your
own kitchen seemingly lost, yet you give kids
you don't even know that incredible experience.
If you can teach them to cook, how come you
can't write down a recipe?"

Shane's teeth clenched; he turned his gaze
away from her and directed it forward out the
limo's front windshield. Colored lights reflect-
ing from the giant advertisements on the Strip
played shadows across his face.

Yikes, she shouldn't have picked at his wound
like that, but he'd riled her up. Rolling around

in her own old hurts hadn't helped her move forward any. All it had served to do was hold her back and limit her world.

"Shane, I'm sorry I said that," she begged. "I had a really difficult relationship with my mother and when I saw those kids—"

"It's none of my business," Shane interrupted, but he kept his eyes forward. His jaw ticked.

"Exactly," she agreed. "Let's just have a fun evening as colleagues and we don't have to talk about anything serious."

"How long do we have to stay?"

How did this evening get off to such a sour start so fast? Audrey answered her own question. Unlike everyone she'd ever known in her life, including herself, Shane Murphy wasn't someone who pretended everything was okay.

Alright, Shane thought as he helped Audrey out of the limo at Caesars Palace. She wanted a fun evening…he'd give her a fun evening. He could use one himself. But what constituted fun? He didn't know anymore. Did she?

As they were ushered onto the night's red carpet, he didn't have time to ponder the question. A solid wall of arms aiming camera lenses stretched for yard upon yard toward the new club's entrance. The camera flashes were like endless exploding fireworks blinding guests as they promenaded down the long carpet.

Shane spotted some film actors, musicians and sports stars among the lineup. Each grouping stopped at a few interview stations set up for reporters to try to grab a sound bite that news outlets could use with the photos.

"This is a big whoop," Shane said as he leaned down toward Audrey by his side while they took slow steps to keep pace with the crowd. He knew that with her job, she'd probably been involved with extravaganzas like these many times. "Have you orchestrated high-rolling shindigs like this?"

"Well, you know loud and glitzy isn't Girard style," she replied, both of them having to raise their voices to be heard over the festivities. "But we've done red carpets on a smaller scale. Like for charity fundraisers. You?"

"The opening in LA was all-out glam. In New York, we built ourselves up slowly with invitation-only nights. But to have an impact on Los

Angeles, we figured we'd better go full tilt. A lot of press. Not that I did anything but get out of the kitchen to put my arms around people for photos."

Conversation was coming easier than he'd thought it would with Audrey after that brisk exchange in the limo. Small talk was hardly Shane's specialty but he had to admit it was nice to get out and Audrey looked killer in that shiny dress. He was tempted to reach out and run his fingers along the fabric. And what was underneath it.

"What do we have planned for *our* opening?" He continued their chat between the two co-workers who were not the slightest bit attracted to each other.

"We're doing a number of what I'm calling parties." She looked up to him in the shoulder-to-shoulder throng on the carpet. "An opening night at the restaurant with invited guests. Another opening for investors. A late-night bash for our social media followers. Brunch for the press. A dance party at the pool."

"Shane Murphy!" A reporter thrust her microphone in his face. "What can you tell us about the new Shane's Table opening at the Girard?"

He turned on the hundred-watt smile he only took out of his back pocket when it was absolutely necessary. "Fresh food. Craft cocktails. A fiesta every night."

"Shane, who are you with tonight?" another reporter probed as the cameras pointed at them.

"This is Audrey Girard, director of public relations for the Girard hotels." The Girard family had a renowned name but, apparently, her face wasn't as instantly recognizable to the press as his was.

"Are you two a couple?" the first reporter interrogated with glee while the photographers went at them.

"Nah, she's out of my league," Shane quickly retorted.

Audrey blushed.

Which was, of course, so out-of-control cute he wanted to scoop her up and demand Caesars Palace's best suite. There he'd lay her down on a bed fit for a Roman emperor and do things to her that would certainly make her blush some more.

"Come on Shane, you look smitten!" the second reporter persisted. Shane suddenly realized he hadn't been hiding his pull toward Audrey as well as he'd thought he had.

Audrey stepped in with, "The Murphy family of restaurants and the Girard family of hotels are excited to continue our professional collaboration here in the great city of Las Vegas." She stretched her hand out toward Shane in an exaggerated gesture of a professional handshake. He took hers and they pivoted to the cameras for a perfect shot that the photographers gobbled up.

"Mission accomplished." She lifted on tiptoe to whisper this in his ear as they proceeded through the nightclub's tall entrance doors.

Shane and Audrey took in the totality of Big Top, a circus-themed nightclub. They looked up to the swaths of heavy red and gold fabrics draped across the ceiling to make the enormous space look more like a circus tent and less like the arena its size could accommodate.

The entrance had led them to an elevated level of the club. Down on the ground floor, thousands of revelers danced to a pounding rhythm. From a center booth that shot yellow, pink and green light beams in every direction, a deejay commanded the crowd though his micophone, "Let's get this party started, Las Vegaaaas!"

It was rhetorical, because he need only glance around to see that the revelry was well underway.

Gigantic cages hung by chains from the ceiling held dancers whose bodies were painted to look like circus animals. A tall lioness in one cage, a muscular tiger in another, and two painted as parrots in a third swayed to the music, deeply into their own rhythms.

Right beside where Audrey and Shane were standing, a trapeze artist clad in a black-and-white polka-dot leotard swung past them on her way to the other end of the cavernous space where she perched on a landing. At the same time, a male counterpart swung back toward Audrey and Shane. Audrey gawked as he flew by them. "Fantastic."

"Who has a vision for a club like this?" Shane nodded in amazement. "This is astonishing creativity."

Somebody conceived of this, and these days he couldn't even put together a simple ceviche.

A hostess dressed like a lion tamer in a top

hat, red tailcoat, tiny shorts and lace-up boots showed them to one of the plush booths that ringed this level of the club. "Run away and join the circus," she said as she handed them a cocktail menu.

A waitress, in the same top hat plus bra and shorty shorts took their order for the "lion juice" that Shane picked for them, a multi-liquored concoction they'd feel awful from the next day if they drank more than one. Shane wasn't much of a drinker and he noticed Audrey wasn't, either. He'd keep an especially close watch on himself tonight. Drunken unwanted advances toward Audrey would be a big no-no.

After sipping and people-watching, Shane suggested they explore the rest of the club. One level down, photo booths captured guests wearing costumes and props that had been provided. Audrey put on a clown's red nose and curly orange wig while Shane mimed swallowing a pretend flaming sword made of plastic.

They walked away giggling at the instant photos they were handed.

"Let's dance," he suggested when they reached the ground floor.

He maneuvered them into the belly of the dance floor, which was jam-packed with partyers.

The deejay boomed out his directive, "Las Vegaaaas! Fists up, hearts open!" The crowd obeyed as everyone lifted an arm in the air and they undulated as one to the throbbing beat. *Fists up, hearts open.*

Shane and Audrey danced. And danced. And danced some more, until they were sweating. There were some seriously good-looking people in the mass around them. Buff guys in tight shirts and women in dresses the size of postage stamps. But Shane's eyes were only interested in Audrey. How stunning she looked with her hair loose and tousled, sweat glistening on her skin, her golden eyes that gazed up at him.

They writhed and wriggled against each other in uninhibited dancing that almost ought to be called something else. Sobriety notwithstanding, it still took every fiber of Shane's being not to steal Audrey into an embrace, not to claim her lips. Which wasn't allowed.

But in that moment he experienced a freedom, one he'd never felt with Melina nor since. *Hearts open*, the deejay had commanded.

A sudden clearing in Shane's personal raincloud allowed him to see light in a way he hadn't in a long, long time.

CHAPTER SIX

"I DON'T KNOW if it's a good idea for me to take charge of Shane's publicity," Audrey confessed to her dad as they inspected one of the newly finished guest rooms. The various crews would be coming through to give their okays on everything, but Daniel liked to take a look at each of his rooms himself. As he'd taught Audrey, even the tiniest detail can bring a guest back for another stay or make them choose never to return.

"Why?" Daniel asked as he jimmied the windows and checked the sills to make sure they were completed to the specifications.

"I'm uncomfortable around him. He's so...intense." Audrey lay down on one of the beds as a Las Vegas visitor might after a full night on the town. Which was exactly what she'd had. Staying out until almost dawn last night at Big Top with Shane, it was no wonder she was groggy today. In any case, she enjoyed the comfortable mattress for a moment under the guise of quality control.

"You and Shane did great last night," Daniel said, "with your appearance at Caesars Palace."

"How would you know how *we* did, or didn't, do?" Audrey propped up on her elbows while continuing her sprawl on the bed. "He's the celebrity."

Daniel took his phone out of his pocket and tapped in. "It was on the gossip sites this morning." He read from his phone, "'Formerly reclusive star chef Shane Murphy seems to have come out from hiding, tearing up the town with petite hotel powerhouse Audrey Girard. Though they insisted their dealings were of a professional nature only, the pair were their own three-ring circus dirty dancing the night away at Big Top. From the way they had eyes only for each other, we see a unification that might go past the contracts.'"

"Dirty dancing? Eek." Audrey sat up, and opened and shut the drawers in the nightstand that, like the headboard, were finished in a shiny black veneer. It wasn't a lie, though. She and Shane did dance, booty shake, twerk, gyrate, rub up against each other and do every still-legal thing people could do on a dancefloor last night, lost in the music and the crowd.

And therein lay the issue. Of course, they looked like a couple to an outside eye. It was a struggle even for *her* to believe they weren't more than professional partners after the whole magical evening.

"The point was to get Shane photographed out in the nightlife. Not to start gossip about his dating life."

"What's that old saying—any publicity is good publicity?" Daniel chimed in.

"I guess it's all good for the bottom line," she reasoned.

Had she seen attractive widower Shane Murphy out in Las Vegas with a young woman she, too, would have assumed they were out on a date.

In reality, they were both unattached. Audrey hadn't thought of her status as single for a long time. She'd settled into this vague vision of a future with Reg, one that demanded nothing of her. A future she could play out in her mind before it had even begun.

Last night wouldn't have been a problem if she'd been out with Reg. They'd look like a couple, pretend to be in love if it was for the cameras and then get right back to their agreed-upon friendly companionship. All previously plotted and outlined and tied up with a ribbon.

Whereas, with Shane, even being in the same room with him set her off questioning the limitations she had carefully defined for her life.

Daniel inspected the teal and hunter green fabric of the curtains, drawing them open and closed to make sure they slid properly.

There was so much her sweet dad didn't know. He wasn't aware that his wife's pregnancy was accidental. Wasn't aware just how much Jill never wanted to have a child, because she'd never told him. Or that when she did become pregnant and Daniel's happiness prevented her from any option other than having the baby, she didn't know what to do with Audrey once she was born.

Jill had treated Audrey like a chore. She would make sure the nanny gave Audrey a bath at night, she'd take her to the doctor if she was sick and sought out good schools for her. In other words, she fulfilled the job requirements of a mother.

Her mother had *managed* her daughter's upbringing. But she had never been a part of it. Like the time with the birthday cake. She had never let Audrey need her. Daniel had tried his best to fill in the gaps, which Audrey was grateful for, but there was no substitute for a mother's love and involvement.

It was only years later that Audrey would come to understand that her mother had suffered from crippling depression. And that the pills and alcohol she'd used to numb her pain only took her even further away.

A distant mother who wasn't warm or watchful, Jill had died without letting her daughter love and dote on her, either.

It was no surprise, then, that Audrey was committed to spending her adulthood with her walls firmly erected.

Argh, she wished Shane Murphy would stop complicating matters by putting those convictions to the test!

Audrey slid open the room's clothes closet to make sure everything was in order. "I just wonder if we shouldn't hire someone to work with Shane. You know, not get ourselves so mixed up in his personal business." That dancing last night surely felt, uh, personal.

"I think we're down to the wire here. And he's comfortable with you. It's what he wants."

"Yeah but…"

"Listen, I don't want to worry you, but I met with Wayne and Suzanne this morning." The building contractor and the hotel general manager. "Because of the teardown and rebuild we had to do in the north corridor, the zeroes to the twelves on all four floors aren't going to be ready in time for the opening."

Audrey's eyes widened in alarm. "For our grand opening, the whole hotel won't be fully opened?"

"Our other guests won't be inconvenienced, but it does mean we can't take reservations to capacity."

"But the first quarter of revenues isn't going to be what we hoped it would be."

"Which is why I don't think this is the time to let anything out of our hands. Who knows what we'd really get if we hire someone to handle Shane. We know you'll do the job right."

Now her concerns seemed trivial. That with Reg it would be easy to pretend there was something between them. And that with Shane, even though there was nothing, it felt like something. Because when she was with him, there was definitely not nothing.

She'd confessed the same thing to Shane earlier. Not the real Shane, of course, with whom she'd had an electrifying evening with at the club. No, it had been daybreak this morning in her bungalow over a cup of herbal tea when she was having that conversation with cardboard Shane. Who was so easy to talk to.

After that, she was disgusted with herself for having yet another tête-à-tête with a photograph, and actually got out of bed and turned the display around so that she didn't have to see his expressive eyes or look at the powerful hands that had traveled down her back when they were dancing last night. Or notice those solid thighs that she had boogied around and between as the dancing got more and more wild. With the photo turned around, all she had to see was a white cardboard outline of the enthralling man she couldn't stop thinking about.

Then the weirdest thing happened. When she woke up after conking out for a few hours' sleep, the cutout had turned around. She opened her eyes to Shane's welcoming face wishing her a good morning. Either she'd been sleep-walking and turned the photo around during the night, or the display was possessed with demonic abilities.

In any case, with this bad news about the con-struction delays, Audrey couldn't back down. She'd have to go through with the plans. She could handle it. Absolutely. As long as she didn't let it occur to her that she might want to spend every moment of the rest of her life with Shane Murphy.

Making a quick mental list, firstly she'd defi-nitely need to keep her recollections away from yesterday afternoon at Feed U. How when she witnessed the smiles he brought to the faces of the kids, she thought sincerely for the very first time about what the joys of having a child might be. His praise for them made her ponder what it would be like to encourage someone, and to find pleasure in their achievement.

Second, it would not be her problem to figure out how to yank Shane out from the shadow he'd been under since his wife's death. Hitting a nightclub and playing around with the kids was fine, but most of his time seemed to be spent in his own personal prison. He needed to live fully again, to unlock the inventiveness and skill he'd bound in chains. But that was another task that would categorically *not* be on her to-do list.

Third, to make this work, she most certainly wouldn't be participating in evenings like last night again. Like when he ever-so-slowly slid his enormous hands down the bare spine her halter dress revealed, which was a sensation that would now rank in her personal hall of fame greatest moments of her life. Possibly even surpassing his slither against her in the sea ten years ago.

As long as there was none of *any* of that, she'd be fine.

Shane was already at the rooftop pool complex when Audrey and Daniel came up to meet him.

This was where they'd tape one of the segments for Shane's TV special and also where they'd hold the press brunch. The area was quite a contrast to the no-frills employee pool. Audrey loved the grandeur of what was dubbed Maurice's Club, named after her grandfather who began the Girard hotel business.

This massive rooftop pool area was to be one of the highlights of Hotel Girard Las Vegas and she hoped it would be a big draw for guests. The day club pool scene in Vegas was a major part of the visit for the under thirty-five crowd. A day in the fresh air with cocktails, music and lots and lots of barely clad flesh brought people out in droves. And especially as a boutique hotel with no casino, many other events would take place at the pool, as well. She and her father had known that they would have to create a truly spectacular daytime venue to compete with what their giant neighbors had already established. And they had.

Audrey was thrilled to see the superb designs come to life. The area utilized a full L-shape of two sides of the roof of the square property.

Glass guard rails enclosed the entire perimeter, which allowed a fun fifth-story view of Las Vegas Boulevard and the Strip.

The two swimming pools mirrored each other, both a sensuous pear shape. The narrower ends of the pools were linked together with a bridge. Guests would be able to walk over the bridge and interact with people in the water while swimmers could coast underneath to move from pool to pool. A crew was at work tiling both of the pools with turquoise glass mosaic.

As was the custom for pool clubs, a stage for well-known deejays and guest performers was under construction.

The landscapers had already planted rows of palm trees to define the club space. On the roof, round concrete platforms with two steps up to each level formed a staircase of patios where plush lounge chairs and small tables would be utilized by sun worshippers. Turquoise and fuchsia pink were the base colors for the pool decor. Coordinating umbrellas would provide shelter.

Six hot tubs were dotted across the roof. At the corner where the two sides of the roof met sat a section of pod-like structures, each of which had three walls and a canvas roof. These were the poolside cabanas for those seeking a luxury experience. With a curtain to draw for privacy, the interiors were to be equipped with a refrigerator to keep refreshments cold all day and wiring for electronics. Waitstaff would be shuttling in buckets of icy beers, tiered towers of seafood, silver trays of deserts. In essence, whatever the guest wanted, Hotel Girard would be able to provide. And charge for.

"Fabulous, sir." Shane reached to shake Daniel's hand after he had taken in the scope of this important hotel feature. "I walked through a couple of months ago, but now it's really taken shape."

"I've sent an eblast to our loyalty club members with an exclusive offer," Audrey announced. "Two nights in a suite and two days of cabanas and cocktails at an attractive price."

"Let's hope we've got a winner here on all

fronts," Daniel said. "Audrey, fill us in on the press brunch."

One of the events for the grand opening was to be a full press tour of the hotel followed by mini massages from the spa staff and concluding with a brunch.

"We'll do the buffet here." Audrey pointed to the outer corner of the L, "that way everyone gets a great view."

"Good," Daniel approved.

"Shane had some helpful recommendations that we do fruit kebobs and breakfast pastries so that guests can eat standing or sitting on loungers, rather than food that needs tables or a fork and knife."

Shane lowered his aviator sunglasses and aimed his dark eyes at her, "I never said that."

"Yeah, you did," Audrey insisted. "When you also suggested we do a flavored-coffee bar and mini smoothies."

"Those are good ideas. Not mine."

Oops, Audrey winced. She hadn't had that conversation with *this* Shane! That was from a late-night brainstorming session she'd had with clever cardboard Shane.

"Great, that's what we'll go with," she quickly tried to cover. Shane wrinkled his eyebrows at her and then used one finger to secure his sunglasses back in place.

"What about the TV taping? You're shooting part of it up here?" Daniel asked.

"Can I snap a few pictures of you on my phone just to think about placement?" Audrey asked Shane. Photo shoots and TV segments with Shane at different locations in the hotel would showcase the property and help promote his iconic image.

Right now in his aviators, chef's coat and with those leather cords wrapped around his wrist, he had image to spare. He was so downright sexy she almost couldn't believe what her eyes saw through the phone's camera. Yes, photos of him would appeal to everyone on earth. Women would want to be *with* him and men would want to *be* him.

This was the man she had rubbed up against in the club last night. She couldn't have had a premonition of what it would feel like to be out in public with him. She had no way of knowing that he'd swirl her into a vortex where the rest of the world disappeared.

But she was not about to let any true feelings for Shane find an opening in the barricade she had built. Feelings could only lead to pain. Feelings only got a person into trouble.

"Were you thinking of doing a segment from the stage?" Daniel pointed to the raised area still being constructed.

"I was." Audrey snapped back to business. "But now I wonder if we shouldn't do it on the bridge between the pools."

"I'm not wearing a bathing suit." Shane made a slicing motion with his hand to indicate his limits. Daniel and Audrey laughed.

"Although, come on, that would be funny if we had you rise up from the pool like a god of the sea," Audrey bounced back. A sliver shot up her spine remembering that swish of wet Shane against wet Audrey in St. Thomas. "Seriously though, let's do get you out of the chef's coat for some of this. Maybe crisp white casual clothes. It will be perfect framing with you on the bridge, the pools gleaming, the Strip in the background."

Daniel elbowed his daughter affectionately. "Nice."

Shane nodded, too.

Audrey fixated on the bridge. On crossing a bridge. Passing from one reality in space and time. Into another.

"I had a nice time last night," Shane's voice called out to Audrey when she was on her third lap of the evening.

No! Not again! With twenty-four hours in a day, why were she and Shane in the employee pool at the exact same time again?

She asked the black sky for an answer but didn't receive one.

Tonight, Audrey was so tired she didn't even have the energy to run away from him. She just wanted to do her laps in peace, but he swam to meet her as she reached the edge of the pool.

"I had a really, really, really nice time last night at Big Top," he repeated.

Audrey squeezed some water out of her hair. "I did, too." Surely there was no harm in admitting that.

"I've been thinking all day about the imagination it took to conceive of that nightclub. While I'm beating my head against the wall in an empty kitchen, waiting for something to happen that just isn't coming."

"Would you be better off in the hustle and bustle of one of your restaurants?" she inquired with genuine concern. For people who didn't know each other very well, she and Shane seemed to cut to the quick with some brutally honest conversations. Which filled her with a mix of terror and emancipation she didn't know how to process. Her connection with him was unlike anything she'd ever experienced before.

"I'm sure you've been in one of your hotel restaurants during the dinner service?"

Audrey nodded. It was like a hospital emergency room.

"Everything happens so fast," he said, "you're firing on all cylinders. Orders are being barked, dishes are being finished and sent out. Cooks and waiters are yelling. Dishes are clattering. It's blistering hot and ear-splittingly loud. It can be the greatest rush in the world, but it can drain the life out of you."

"It must be very hectic."

"I used to thrive on it."

He pushed off the side and swam a lap. Audrey followed. With him a foot taller than her, she finished well behind.

"I've fizzled out. Nothing sparks me up anymore." They each held on to the edge of the pool.

He used two fingers on his free hand to move some strands of wet hair off her face. The tender touch across her forehead was in stark contrast to what he was saying to her.

She wasn't sure if he was asking for advice. "The ecstasy is gone." The pain in his eyes lasered toward her and struck at her heart. "I'm dead to it. I don't know how to reclaim it."

"But at Feed U, with the kids…"

"Oh, come on. Cutting up kooky-umbers for a bunch of cute munchkins who think I'm a rock star. How hard is that?"

It was impossible to reconcile the two Shanes. How could he deny the twinkle in his eye and the enthusiasm in his voice when he made salad with those kids and told them about the vitamins and minerals in leafy greens? That didn't mesh with the imprisoned man who couldn't break out of his own shackles.

"What would inspire you?" Audrey chastised herself for having thoughts on how to solve his problems. It wasn't her job to get involved, although if he was going to finish the cookbook, he needed to confront what was holding him back. "You mentioned some old friends you know in Vegas that you haven't been to see. Do you think that might help?"

"Maybe." She could tell he wanted to tell her something else. He started to speak and then stopped himself. "There's something I've only just figured out."

"Do you want to tell me what it is?"

The pool water became still as they remained in place.

He stalled.

Exhaled.

Raked his hair.

Eyes darted out to the distance. Left to right as if he were defending his territory.

Then he looked to her.

But couldn't bear it so he returned to surveying nothingness.

"I didn't…"

Without finishing the thought, he took off for another lap across the pool. Audrey noticed the speed and ferocity with which he swam.

When he returned, his voice was tight and low.

"I didn't love her."

"Who?"

"My wife." Shane shook his head back and forth as if he himself was in total disbelief. His words were like bullets. "I. Didn't. Love. Her."

Suffering poured out of his eyes as they met hers.

Audrey instantly wanted to reach out and hold him while he cried out all the agony he had inside. Which was strange because that wasn't a gift anyone had ever extended to her. She'd always felt the need to hold herself together in front of other people. Any tears Audrey shed had been when she was alone. But she wanted to feel Shane's teardrops on her skin.

At the moment, though, he looked untouchable so she didn't dare move. Muscles spasmed in his arms and shoulders. Which convinced her that they weren't having a conversation. She just happened to be in the pool while he was having an emotional breakthrough.

But she *was* here. "Do you want to talk about it?"

Silence.

He pushed off for another lap. She followed and met him at the other side. Squinting, he said, "We had gone to her mother's cabin in upstate New York for a couple of days. To me, the trip was a sort of last ditch effort to make it better with her."

"Did it help?"

"No." He bristled as if arrows of memory were attacking him from every angle. "We were not a fit. We were just living out the whim we had acted on. It was growing more obvious with every day that we had nothing substantial between us."

"And?" Audrey encouraged him to keep talking.

"A torrential storm blew through and we were snowed in," he said as if he was seeing the blizzard right in front of him. "Instead of that being romantic and cozy, it only pointed out the chasm between us even more clearly. I really couldn't take it anymore."

He stopped abruptly, working something through in his own mind.

"What happened after that?"

His lower jaw jutted out as he continued processing his thoughts.

"I told her that as soon as the weather cleared and we could get back to the city I was going to move out of our apartment." He squeezed his eyes shut and swallowed back a breath. "I'm sure she wasn't surprised. But she put on a jacket and went out the cabin's door. I thought she was just going out to the porch for air until I heard the car engine."

Audrey wrapped her hand around the leather cording that enveloped Shane's wrist, unable to censor herself from wanting to offer some tangible support. He violently shook her hand off.

"Visibility was terrible," he said as his head fell forward toward his chest. "I don't know how she even pulled the car out of the driveway. Sheer will, I suppose. I sat staring into my cup of coffee, lost in thought. And sadness. I'd intended to make it work with her. I thought I had tried."

"I'm so sorry," Audrey muttered. She'd had no idea that Shane had been unhappy in his marriage. How many times had he told this story, and when he did, what got included and what got left out? What was he editing out now?

"By the time I comprehended what she was doing, I ran to the front door to stop her, but she was gone. I'd been so caught up in my own head, I'd let her go. Within a few miles of the cabin she crashed into a telephone pole."

"You couldn't have predicted what would happen," Audrey interjected.

He leaned his elbows on the ledge of the pool and held his face in his hands. Sheer sorrow poured out of him. "The highway patrol had advised staying off the roads. I should have chased after her. I couldn't protect her from the mistake of our marriage, but I should have shielded her from harm. I was her husband."

"It doesn't sound like she would have listened at that moment."

"I was her *husband*. Who didn't love her." He gulped in some air. Jutted out his chin again and then retracted it. Anguish roiled through his voice. "I didn't love her. I've never said that out loud."

Drops of water trickled down from his hair onto his back. His voice rose. "I DIDN'T LOVE HER!"

CHAPTER SEVEN

"LET'S GO FOR a ride," Shane said to Audrey when she arrived at the kitchen's delivery dock. He'd texted her early this morning and asked her to meet him.

"Where are we going this time?"

"You want to take the bike?" he pointed to his nearby motorcycle.

"I most certainly do not want to take the bike," she scrunched up her nose.

"I know, I know, you're not dressed for it." He repeated what she had said the last time when she wouldn't put the helmet on. Indeed, in yet another prim business dress, today in navy, and her high heels, Audrey was not going to straddle his Yamaha. That was okay. He was only teasing her. With a wave, he opened the passenger door of the Jeep for her to get in.

"Where are you taking me?" She tried again

as she swung into the seat and put on her dark sunglasses.

"Somewhere that worked for me in the past," he closed the car door.

"Okay," she kindly agreed.

Shane cranked up his rock 'n' roll and took off. They traveled far away from the Strip and the center of the town. Soon the gorgeous Spring Mountains of the Mojave Desert didn't have to compete with the pizzazz of the city. He hadn't taken this drive in a long time but it was one he knew by heart. It was good to be out on the open road, silent but for his music, with Audrey beside him.

It was true about getting things off your chest.

After last night in the pool with Audrey, when Shane had said aloud for the first time that he had never loved Melina, he drove home with agonizing remembrances banging through his head.

As soon as he got to his apartment, he'd crashed facedown on his bed. He'd punched his pillows, screamed and even wept. Cried for the first time since Melina's death, until he finally emptied what had seemed a bottomless well of grief.

Then, much to his surprise, he felt lighter. His outpouring didn't minimize the tragedy of Melina's death. It did nothing to alleviate his guilt, either about not preventing her accident or about not loving her. Yet it had never before occurred to him that he hadn't been able to get it all said.

Taking the words from inside his brain and putting them into his mouth gave them a perimeter. The words had a beginning and they had an end. It was his horror to face head-on, but it was much better than carrying it around in his gut like a lead weight.

The last thing he could remember thinking about before he finally fell asleep was Audrey in the pool placing her hand on his arm to offer comfort. It was somehow because of her that he was able to face his truth.

The first thing he thought of when he woke up this morning was seeing her again as soon as possible.

The second thought was of Josefina, his longtime pal who reminded him of his grandmother Lolly. It was shameful that he'd been spending this much time in Vegas and hadn't gone out to see her yet. Previously, if he'd been anywhere near the American Southwest he'd made a point to connect with her. If there was any hope for him, he needed to stop cutting himself off from what might help set him straight.

After letting out his secret about Melina, Josefina was the next bridge to cross.

Eventually, they reached the left turn at the corner Laundromat. Everything looked exactly the same as it had when he was here last. Children played ball in the street. Small houses were painted in pastel colors. Then it was a right at the local *mercado*. A banner hung from an old church building advertising worship services in Spanish. With another right turn, he pulled into the parking lot of Casa Josefina.

"What's this?" Audrey asked while unbuckling her seat belt. She smoothed down her hair, which had been swirling in the open-topped Jeep. Navigating the graveled parking lot was no easy maneuver for her in her work heels. Shane dashed to her side to provide a stable arm, which she gratefully grabbed hold of. His chest swelled with a sort of pride as he helped her into the small adobe building.

"Remember how you suggested that I reach out to important people in my life who I've been cut off from? I'm taking your advice."

"Shane, *mi amor*!" Josefina noticed them as soon as they came through the restaurant's door. She rushed over. "I am so happy to see you. Why has it taken you so long to visit me?"

Was the answer that shame and regret had kept him from those he cared about?

All he could do now was try to move forward. Shane embraced Josefina, wrapping his arms around her slim body. Josefina had been something of a mentor, and she was certainly a true friend. They kissed each other on both cheeks.

"How are the grandbabies?"

"Paulo is riding his tricycle day and night. Olivia is learning to walk."

"If there's anything Josefina loves more than cooking, it's her family," Shane said to Audrey by way of introduction. "This is my friend Audrey."

That sounded awkward the minute it came out of his mouth. Audrey wasn't exactly his friend.

His introduction didn't matter to Josefina, who sized Audrey up with a sparkle in her eyes and a toothy grin that told Shane she was thinking the obvious. That Audrey was a love interest he had brought to her restaurant.

"Que linda," she complimented Audrey. Pretty, she surely was. Then Josefina murmured under her breath to Shane, *"Finalmente."*

"No, Josefina," Shane protested with a chuckle. "Audrey is actually a coworker." He realized he should have asked Audrey ahead of time if she wanted to be introduced with her last name. Everyone in Vegas knew the Girards had purchased the old Royal Neva. Maybe Audrey wasn't in the mood for a barrage of questions, so he didn't mention it.

"Coworker? I see." Josefina shot him a mischievous smile of disbelief. "You have come to eat? Please." She gestured into her small restaurant.

The dining room was dark but strung with Christmas lights that blinked year-round. Half of the dark wood booths were filled with midafternoon diners. Come dinnertime, people would be waiting an hour for a table to sample

Josefina's Oaxacan specialties. Attracting a mix of locals and tourists, the restaurant was both a neighborhood joint and a foodie pilgrimage.

With the raised dais in the corner decorated with hanging piñatas and streams of Mexican flags, the restaurant also sometimes served as a wedding chapel. Josefina was an ordained marriage officiant. After all, this was Vegas and that designation had been known to come in handy.

"I need to take a call." Audrey swiped her phone.

Meanwhile, everything Shane wanted to say to Josefina spilled out. About being stymied in his efforts to nail down the cookbook recipes. How blocked in general he was. The disconnection and isolation he'd been feeling.

Josefina patted him on the back. "Now you have come to see me. And you are with this magical woman. Change is in the wind."

Just what he'd been thinking on the car ride over.

"Come, *chicos*, I am starting a pot of mole negro. Mole is so complicated it takes your mind off of your troubles." She took Shane by the arm and turned to Audrey. "You put your phone away, *linda*, and come to my kitchen."

Josefina gave them aprons, which they tied on. Audrey couldn't do anything about her business garb but pulled her hair back into a ponytail with a band she found in her purse. "Toast the onions and garlic in the frying pan," Josefina instructed her. "Shane, the chilies have been soaking. Now we puree them."

Her small kitchen with its well-worn supplies and equipment was nothing like the huge operation Shane was running at his restaurants. Everything that came out of this kitchen was flavored with love, something he needed to remember if he wanted to stay sincere to his own mission of treating each diner as if the meal had been prepared just for them.

He enjoyed the heavy crank of Josefina's old-fashioned food mill as he used it to separate the skins from the flesh of the chilies.

Grandma Lolly had had one just like it. Shane wondered if it was in the stack of old pots and pans of hers he had under his desk at the restaurant. He hadn't worked with Lolly's things in a long time. Maybe that would help him get back what he'd lost.

Audrey dutifully moved the chopped onion and minced garlic around the scorching hot skillet. She'd told Shane she didn't know how to cook. But she was a hard worker, he could tell that from all she did for her family's company.

And he couldn't help gawking at how lovely she looked as she performed the task with a determined concentration.

"Josefina is from Oaxaca in Southwestern Mexico," Shane explained to Audrey over the sizzle of her pan. "The area is known for some of the most complex food in that country. Moles are sauces that have dozens of ingredients."

Josefina continued to give them small steps working toward the completion of her mole. Pan fry the sesame seeds. Then the pecans. When they have cooled down, pulverize them in a spice grinder. "That's right, *mijo*." She caressed Shane's back with the endearment used for a son. "This is what we do. We get absorbed in the work. The miracle is in the work."

Fry the raisins. Fry the plantains. Shane did appreciate the meditation of the tasks.

Josefina's two staff cooks filled orders for diners in the same small space with them while upbeat Spanish music played from an old radio. When the sauce had reached the point where it needed to simmer, Josefina served Shane and Audrey a plate of chicken topped with the last of her mole negro from the previous batch. "It is still my top seller," Josefina said, talking shop to Shane.

He and Audrey stood in a corner of the kitchen, two forks digging into the same plate.

Audrey's eyes lit up at the flavor of the dense, spicy, almost black sauce atop the simple grilled chicken.

"What do I taste that's familiar?" she asked.

"I'll give you three guesses," Shane teased. He tilted his head to Josefina, "Sugar here has got a big-time sweet tooth. Maybe this is the way we'll get her to eat chicken."

"Chocolate!" Audrey exclaimed. "Wow, is that good. Chocolate on chicken. But it's not really sweet, is it? It has layers of flavor. Brilliant."

"This girl is full of life, yes, Shane?" Josefina arched her eyebrows knowingly at him.

"I told you—" Shane gently squeezed Josefina's shoulder "—she and I are business partners."

Josefina flashed her playful grin. "Maybe it's a different kind of partner you need, *mijo*."

After Josefina packed them some food to take, it was time to go. In the dining room, Shane hugged her. Then Josefina embraced Audrey as if she'd known her for her entire life. "When my Xavier died," she murmured to Audrey, although Shane was able to hear, "I could not come back to myself. It took a lot of time and a lot of patience to heal."

Shane knew Josefina was talking about him. Audrey looked Josefina in the eyes, unsure what to make of the unexpected intimacy. Then Audrey blurted, "My mother died three years ago. She was fifty-three."

"Ah, so you and Shane have your tragedies to bind you."

Audrey blinked heavily, not having been prepared for Josefina's quick analysis.

"These two want to get married." Josefina pointed to a couple waiting on the dais who were dressed in jeans but adorned with feather boas, sequined bowler hats and neon-plastic sunglasses. "Vegas, baby."

In the Jeep on the way back, Shane had a crystal-clear thought.

The pace he'd been keeping coupled with Melina's death had removed him from the only alchemy he'd ever known. By combining ingredients the way a painter would mix paints, he used to be able to find a new color. A holy formation that wasn't on the earth before.

After the devastation of Melina's death and the self-reproach that tore pieces of his flesh away day by day, those brushes with divinity stopped coming. Really the process had been shutting down for years. His relationship with Melina had been a chore. The lust, if that's what it would be called, that drew them together had long since faded. Pretending to keep up the relationship with someone who was essentially a stranger had done nothing more than wear him out.

His business had already been sagging before her death. He had lost steam. Too much fame, too many accolades, too many projects at too young an age to handle them. A lightbulb that burned too brightly. The restaurants had gotten to the point where they were running themselves, but he wasn't doing anything to keep them fresh and vital. He'd turned the kitchens over to his executive chefs, who were inventing the specials and new menu ideas that he should have been. When he crept into the New York or LA restaurants, it was usually to cook for an event or a group of VIPs that Reg had courted. Perhaps the Murphy brothers had gone as far as they could without that next insight into the future.

Then Reg was approached by the Girards with this Vegas idea. Which seemed like an ideal location with Shane's predilection for Spanish cooking and Vegas's world-class dining. Maybe this could be it. Las Vegas could turn everything around. Great food was available here. And Audrey was right—he needed to reconnect with people who knew him when he was at his best, like Josefina and his old kitchen mates from Paris, Tino and Loke.

Vegas could be where he found the good luck charm he had misplaced. It could not only revive, but catapult his career. Could he open up his soul again and reunite with the spirit that used to run through him? Was he capable of new heights?

As they sped down the open road away from Josefina's, both Shane and Audrey were absorbed in their own thoughts. She was rerunning Josefina's words to her about how she and Shane had loss to tie them together. Did having something like that in common *really* make people more compatible? Did it define who they were?

What she and Shane seemed to share was a commitment to *not* getting into a relationship after what their pasts had dealt them. Audrey hoped that important similarity itself would carry them through their dealings together.

The sun was beginning to set behind the mountains. "Wow—" Audrey pointed ahead to the horizon "—that's incredibly beautiful."

"Do you have to get back to the hotel? Let's take a longer look," Shane stated rather than asked. At the next turnoff, he drove them farther from the city along a flat road paved through dirt, cactus and other desert flora. Closer to the foot of the mountains, he pulled the car over and shut off the engine. In the peaceful silence of nowhere, Audrey vaguely remembered scenes from mafia movies where thugs would take wise guys out here never to return.

The view of the sunset was otherworldly. Nature was putting on one of her best shows. The noble red mountains with their voluptuous slopes rested calm and proud as darkness descended on them. Beneath the clusters of billowy clouds, the colors in the sky presented stunning layers of blue, purple, orange and yellow.

"That is something, isn't it?" Shane marveled.

"What a strange place Las Vegas is. All that manmade light and sound right in the center of all of this," she swept her arm left to right at the spectacular scenery in front of them.

Las Vegas, *the Meadows* in Spanish, had begun to attract visitors with legalized gambling, and loose requirements for marriage and divorce, in the 1930s. It grew, and continued to grow, into a one-of-a-kind oasis in the desert that the whole world flocked to. A place where people left their troubles at home, and came to play and indulge. As a restaurateur and hotelier, Shane and Audrey were trying to get their own pieces of that promise.

Shane unbuckled his seat belt and leaned back to enjoy the panorama. Audrey did the same. Out of the corner of her eye, she studied him. His striking face with its distinct jawline and beard stubble could almost give the sunset a run for its money. She stiffened at the realization that she hadn't sat in a parked car with a man in years. Not only hadn't she sat with a man in a parked car, she hadn't been anywhere with a man.

What had she become? Just a work bunny who pattered around all day long until she was exhausted enough to go to sleep, only to wake up and do it again? What kind of life was that? What was the end game?

A part of her was very disappointed to lose Reg. Maybe it would have worked out nicely to have the less challenging Murphy as a companion. With Reg, she wouldn't have had to risk getting hurt. Wouldn't have had to ask herself any questions like the ones about authentic love that had begun scrolling through her mind since she'd been spending time with Shane.

But Reg was no longer an option. He'd flown off to share sunsets filled with real feelings.

And here she sat with this red-hot man beside her now. Who was dynamite and could blow her into pieces. His mere being already held too great a power over her. They'd experienced too much together already.

It wasn't only her mind that asked questions when she was around Shane. It was her very essence, her identity, her womanhood, her soul. Those were supposed to be off-limits.

Shane stretched his shoulders back and let out a sigh. The reverberation of his voice made every hair on her body stand on end.

"How do you know Josefina?" Audrey asked to distract herself from the dangerous places her insides were taking her.

Shane smiled while he kept his eyes on the sunset. "Through Diego Reyes, a madman chef in Mexico City. He brought Josefina and me together years ago to create a banquet for his daughter's wedding and we became fast friends."

"She's very loving."

He agreed, "She reminds me of my grandmother Lolly, who taught me how to cook and serve food in the first place."

"What's something you remember learning to cook with Lolly?" Was she putting on her micromanaging hat, as if trying to solve Shane's problems was a way of distancing herself from her own? Every move Shane made and every move she made around him seemed to be calling her out on her own facades, on the lies she'd told herself too many times.

Shane's mouth tipped into a half smile. "Coddle. An old Irish dish she learned from *her* mother. Which can be dull as old shoes but, of course, Great-grandma Peg's recipe was delicious."

"What was her secret?"

"Sorry, Sugar, I'll never tell that one."

Audrey shifted in her seat. It made her itch every time he called her Sugar. She hated it. She loved it.

"When we drove out to Josefina's, you told me that cooking with her had helped you in the past. What did you mean?"

"The way she cooks reminds me that there aren't any shortcuts. Yeah, there's inspiration, but it's only slogging through that gets you where you're going. I'm waiting for a lightbulb to go off in my brain. I've lost my perseverance for the sheer work."

Audrey felt the opposite. All she could do was work, lose herself in detail. In the absence of toil, there was only emptiness.

Idle time was an aching reminder of what she was missing. What she had always been lacking. Deep down, that love she'd never received from her mother was something she'd never stop yearning for.

Her heart spiraled downward in sputters until it reached despair. Then she set her intention and pulled herself back up to the surface as she'd done so many times before.

Asking Shane another question, she threw herself a rope.

"How does a recipe get created?"

"An idea starts to come together in your mind. And then you try it out. And it's not right. You change it around. A little less this, a little more that, let's add in something else. Then you try it again. And again. And again.

Eventually, if you're lucky, you find something that's only yours."

"You'll find your way back." She was sure of it.

Apparently having had enough of that conversation, Shane opened his car door. "Let's get out."

He came around to her side of the car and helped her out. There were no other cars anywhere. They were miles away from town, under the sunset and the hush of nightfall.

With no warning whatsoever, Shane rested one hand on each of Audrey's shoulders. He leaned down and kissed her. His lips pressed against hers with closed-mouthed but adamant force.

Her neck flushed instantly. Having him close to her was a little bit familiar now after their bodies had writhed together with their sexy dancing at Big Top. But he hadn't kissed her that night, and this new intimacy set off alarms in her system.

It was a shock she missed with all of her might when he took his lips away.

Shane let loose a laugh that echoed in the

quiet of the desert. "My apologies. I don't know what the heck I did there."

Audrey's lungs ceased functioning. She was furious at him for having taken his lips from her. All she could seem to want was for him to kiss her again. Oxygen in, carbon dioxide out—she reminded herself of the basic breathing process.

"Come here," he said, filling her with the hope that his mouth would graze hers again. Her eyelids fluttered uncontrollably.

But no. He lifted her up and sat her on the hood of his Jeep. Then hoisted himself onto it, as well. He maneuvered backward so that he could lean back against the glass of the windshield with his legs outstretched on the hood. Then he helped shimmy Audrey backward so that she could do the same.

She somehow didn't care that she was wearing a business dress and heels. His spontaneity was liberating.

Now they were able to continue to watch nature's spectacle with a warm breeze gliding across their faces.

Audrey had to settle herself down. He'd obviously kissed her by mistake. Out of some kind of urge that probably had nothing to do with her. She shouldn't read anything into it.

Maybe sensing Audrey's discomfort, Shane thankfully broke the quiet. "What was Josefina saying to you about tragedies?"

She creased her forehead, not sure what or how much was appropriate to tell Shane. "I told her that my mother died three years ago. Josefina thought that loss was a similarity to share."

Shane chuckled wistfully. "Does it work that way?"

Audrey shook her head. "I was wondering the same thing."

They took in the majesty of the sunset again. The sides of their bodies pressed into each other.

"You didn't love your wife," Audrey mused, "and my mother didn't love me."

"What do you mean your mother didn't love you?"

"She didn't. She suffered from a debilitating depression. I wasn't wanted and she never let me get close." Three or four tears broke their way out of hiding and dripped down Audrey's cheek. "When she was dying of cirrhosis of the liver, she didn't let me near then, either. And I didn't push. I let my dad watch her die while I studied market share statements."

"I let Melina die. I didn't protect her."

"I let my mother die without forcing her to let me care."

"We're quite a pair then."

"So we do have something in common, like Josefina said."

Shane turned himself until he was facing her. He kissed the tears on her face, one by one, ever so lightly. A sigh slipped through her lips.

"So soft," he murmured as he dotted kisses all over her face.

His beard stubble felt exactly as she imagined it would, rasping across her cheeks with a welcome harshness. Filling her with the wholly biological need for contact with something that was wholly male. Something that she'd dared not think of in years.

When his mouth inched down her neck, her head fell backward.

With a flattened palm, he caressed the length of her throat from behind her ear to the swerve of her shoulder. His lips moved under the collar of her dress. In a beat, her back arched to meet him.

Flowering with anticipation, her parted lips waited for him to return upward. As if he knew she couldn't delay a moment longer, his open mouth rejoined hers. A quick succession of kisses was followed by a longer one that melded them into each other.

Her arms reached around his neck. His mouth possessed hers, communicating what she had to hear. She met his every sensation, the kisses swirling deeper, further, quaking both of them at their epicenters.

"What are we doing?" Audrey muttered against his lips as Shane's kisses obscured the purple and orange sky from her view.

He whispered, "Sharing loss."

CHAPTER EIGHT

SHANE SHOVED HIS blanket off and rubbed his bare chest and belly. He knew he needed to get out of bed but the blackout shades had done their job of shielding him from the Nevada morning sun and he was just that comfortable. Soft, soft, soft. Audrey's face. Audrey's hands. Audrey's hair. Audrey's mouth. The word *soft* could be applied to so many of the images that played like a video in his mind.

The sun had set and risen again yet he couldn't concentrate on anything other than the memory of kissing Audrey on the hood of his Jeep yesterday.

Of course, it was totally inappropriate. It was all wrong the way their lips explored each other's like they did. It wasn't thought through. It wasn't smart. It wasn't professional.

But, man, was it a mind-blower.

He hadn't had the desire to kiss a woman that

way in ages. The long, long, slow dance with Audrey's mouth had been totally unexpected. And left him certain that he'd never enjoyed kissing anyone that much.

His kisses with Melina had been different. Their physical encounters had begun with an aggressive hunger that was satisfied only too quickly. No time was taken for savoring.

With Audrey, all Shane could envision was the opposite. Were he to make love with her, which he was not going to do, he'd take all the time in the world. He'd bring her waters from warm to hot, and then keep them at a simmer long before he'd let them reach the boiling point. If he ever got her into his bed, he'd…well, that was never, ever, to happen.

Sure, maybe the time had come for him to start dating again. Though he'd never let a woman all the way back into his life. He couldn't be counted on and wouldn't bestow that unreliability on anybody. No one deserved that. Look what had happened with Melina.

If he did decide to fulfill primitive needs, there were billions of women in the world. Audrey was not an option. She was the most precious creature he'd ever encountered and she deserved the kind of dedication and protection he could never offer. Safeguarding was indeed what she needed after what sounded like a childhood filled with dashed hopes and disappointment. He would deny himself anything not to risk injuring her further.

Not to mention the fact that they were corporate partners and, with any luck, would be for many years to come. Messing with that wasn't a gamble to be taken. Business never mixed with pleasure, and with the stakes as high as they were for both families, no unnecessary chances should be taken.

In fact, he couldn't risk any more brushes with her like yesterday's kissing, or even the other night's dancing. Anything further would take him past the point of no return.

Into the stuff of dreams.

Which could too easily turn to nightmares.

But soaping himself up in the shower, he couldn't help riding on the high of those kisses.

After the drive to the restaurant's kitchen, Shane flipped on the lights with one clear intention.

Moving aside the jumble of odds and ends and files that had been shoved under his desk as they set up the office, Shane found what he was looking for. A big packing box that he had sent himself from New York.

Grandma Lolly's pots and pans were easily his most treasured possessions. An instant smile crossed his lips as he opened the box. Like old friends, those pots and pans were his grounding on this earth. He'd let far too much time go by without visiting these beacons.

"Knock, knock." Audrey's voice called out from the back entrance of the kitchen.

"In here," Shane yelled from his office, which was separated from the kitchen with a smoked-glass partition. She found him sitting in the middle of the floor with the box open in front of him.

How was she always so beautiful? She was the personification of the sunny morning. Her blond hair was shiny and clean, and her pink blouse accentuated her creamy skin. His belly lurched with the appetite to pull her down to the floor and pick up where they left off yesterday at sunset.

"What are you doing down there?"

"These were my Grandma's." He pointed inside the box. "These cooking tools are like someone else's childhood teddy bear. I don't have a memory that goes back further than these do."

He lifted out a skillet. It was crusty and rusted but he caressed it as gently as he had Audrey's glossy hair yesterday. "She taught me my first recipe with this pan."

"What was it?"

"Just fried bread and eggs, but what she taught me was how to not fear fire. How to control it. That's the most basic mastery a cook needs."

Audrey stood in the doorway, listening. His impulse to talk to her about things that were important to him was growing every day. Maybe it was just that he'd cut himself off from everyone for so long, he was relearning how to articulate what was inside.

An internal voice corrected him. It was Audrey in particular Shane wanted to talk to.

"My grandma never had old-lady hands," he continued. "Her skin stayed taut until the day she died."

Now Audrey moved toward him. And even though she was in one of her work outfits, she sat down on the floor next to him.

"She had her fair share of burn scars," he chuckled. "You can't spend a life in the kitchen without those."

He displayed the inside of his right arm for Audrey to see. "That was from buquerones fritos." He used his left hand to point to the biggest welt, which was a good inch and a half. Then he switched to his left arm to show her another choice one. Two, actually, that formed a V shape. "And thank you, coliflor rebozada."

"That's a doozy."

"But for all the cooking and dishwashing and running her diner in Brooklyn, Grandma Lolly had the nicest hands."

Shane took one of Audrey's small hands into his. Maybe his grandma had the second nicest hands. Audrey's were pure. They were pink and rounded rather than bony. The orange nail polish was the only thing that revealed they weren't the hands of a small child.

Without thinking twice, he brought her hand

up toward his mouth, about to deliver a light kiss to each finger. He stopped himself in time.

No more kissing her, he chastised his urge. He must keep things only professional with her. Why was he finding that difficult to remember?

Shane returned Audrey's hand to her lap without a word about his actions. Reaching into the box, he hoisted out Lolly's large cast-iron pot.

"Ah, she taught me so many recipes with this Dutch oven. It was her favorite. Soups and mashes. Summer stews. Winter braises for cold nights." He rubbed the bottom of the pot like it could appreciate his affection. "You know, this pot is really why I'm a chef. This is the first one I used to try to create my own recipes."

He'd ask his grandma if thyme might add a good layer of flavor for mushrooms, or if the sweetness of carrots might enhance a potato puree. She'd lean down and give him a pat on the back with approval when he'd come up with something that tasted good. Years later, when he grew tall, she'd have to stretch up to pat the same spot on him.

And although the Brooklyn diner led to the Lolly's chain and a formidable restaurant business for the family, it was Grandma Lolly's special cash jar, which she diligently added to every week, that sent Shane to culinary school. She'd wanted it that way.

He owed so much to her. She'd hate what he'd turned into. Bitter and washed up at thirty-four years old. Lolly would expect him to dust himself off no matter how great his fall and pull himself back together.

Her small sauce pot was almost warm in his hands. He reached into the box for her knife roll. Which he spread out, and then he touched each blade. They were all dull, but a good sharpening could resurrect them.

Here he was in this humongous state-of-the-art kitchen with every tool and gadget at his disposal, his own equipment and knives the finest in the world, yet he knew that he needed to sharpen his grandmother's knives and pretend he was a young boy in the safe haven of her home kitchen.

He stretched one arm up to his desk and grabbed a pencil and scrap of paper, which he pulled down and handed to Audrey.

"Can you write this down? I'll start with the

holy trinity of green peppers, onions and celery. But not with andouille, we'll use chorizo. And lux it up with lobster..."

Four hours later, Shane finished his sixth version of a Cajun-style paella. "Taste," he said to Audrey, who had been coming and going while she took care of other matters on the property but kept popping in to check his progress.

He spooned some of it into her mouth, noting that feeding her had become his new favorite hobby. She nodded her approval and circled the recipe on the piece of paper that was now covered in scribbles. "It's roasting the garlic that works, and less of it?"

"I think I nailed it." He did a shimmy with his shoulders that made Audrey giggle. He grabbed her arm and pulled her to him for a waltz around the kitchen even though the music was better suited to head banging. He kissed two fingers on his own hand and raised them up toward the ceiling. "Thank you, Grandma."

"You've got it?" Audrey wanted to be certain.

"Ladies and gentlemen, Shane Murphy has finally developed a new recipe."

* * *

If Audrey ever wondered who Shane Murphy was before he lost himself, she had her answer. To watch today as the creative juices flowed back into his hands was something to behold. To experience his earnest sense of hospitality, the way he cared to determine whether every single dash of salt would be pleasing to his diner, was magnificent.

She had been watching a painter at his easel. A composer at the piano. It was inspiring the way a resounding "crap" at any failure was quickly followed by the sizzle of oil in a clean skillet or the dice of a new onion. Labor was how he passed the time while waiting for the muse to tell him how to solve the next problem.

"You, sir, are poetry in motion," she gushed to Shane.

Cardboard Shane, that is.

Back in the shelter of her bungalow she could let out what she'd managed to hold in all day. Namely, her wish against wishes that Shane would hold her, kiss her and dance with her again. When part of her yearning came true and he waltzed her around the kitchen after confirming that his paella was finally perfected, Shane fed her body a lifeblood she was sure she would have perished without.

Now, being totally honest, sitting on her bed with her shoes kicked off, gawking at that cutout that she was so enamored of, she wondered if every suite shouldn't be adorned with one of them, and she could admit her revelation.

She wanted to make love with Shane. The prolonged, slow, "lasts all night" type of love. She wanted to do things with him she'd never experienced. The kind of lovemaking that leaves you exhilarated and sweaty and spent on the bed, unable to get up for work the next day.

Through watching Shane in action today, she could tell that he knew deep things about passion and about satisfaction, about modulation and temperance. She wanted him to teach her.

"Hello…" She almost blushed with embarrassment when she answered Daniel's phone call.

She had a flashing moment of fury at her dad. What she was specifically angry about, she didn't know. About her mother. About the twisted person Audrey had become, who told herself she didn't want to be loved. And didn't want to love in return.

Nothing was really her father's fault. Back when her mother was alive, he had been so focused on just putting one foot in front of the next. Trying to take over the hotels from his own father, who had worked for decades to build their name and reputation. Directing and growing the brand. She couldn't really blame anything on her dad. There was something so innocent about him. He'd never known how bad it had gotten for her, the loneliness and the isolation of day after day with a mother who stayed upstairs in a bedroom that was off-limits to Audrey.

The sound of her dad's voice on the other end of the phone was a perfect reminder that she had no reason to be daydreaming about making love with Shane.

They were, and would remain, colleagues and nothing more. She wouldn't even be spending this much time with him if not for the cookbook and the publicity campaigns. Which were necessary for both families. Time to zip it up, rein it in and put her steely face on. She was more than capable of that. That was classic Audrey Girard.

"Do you want to come by my office for dinner?" Daniel asked her.

"Sorry, I can't. Shane asked me to go out with some chef buddies of his."

"Hmm..." Daniel's voice rose an octave. "Have you leaked it to the press?"

Audrey laughed in surprise that she hadn't thought of that. And why hadn't she? Everything Shane did was supposed to be toward a goal.

But when Shane asked her after his victory in the kitchen if she wanted to meet some old friends of his, she knew it was sincere. That he really wanted her to come along. She just needed to keep on guard.

After her now-customary fashion show in the mirror before she decided on what outfit to wear, a fitted black blouse with a deep scoop neck paired with a full lacy white skirt seemed right for what Shane said would be a chefs' night off. She was just slipping on her heels when there was a knock at the bungalow's door.

"Ready," Audrey called as she grabbed her purse and unlatched the lock to find Shane standing in her doorway.

It seemed the most natural thing in the world to lean into him and kiss hello. Fortunately, she caught herself swerving toward him and pulled back in the nick of time. Those kisses under the sunset last night were a beginner's mistake. Not to be repeated. Let yesterday be a lesson to her.

First and foremost, business partners do not shower each other with kisses. Fine, they got carried away yesterday, but now it was time to back up and get on the correct track. Second, kisses like the ones she had with Shane, the kind that made you crave more and more and more of them, were not on her menu. Kisses could lead to feelings. Feelings might lead to hope. And hope led to heartbreak. She knew that connect-the-dots only too well.

Shane placed his hand on the door in an attempt to open it farther. "Can I look at your bungalow? I haven't seen the interior of a finished one."

"Yeah sure." She gestured him in. But as he lifted his foot over the threshold, she suddenly remembered the cardboard cutout of him that had become part of her decor. She surely didn't want him to see that she had it in her room. Propped directly facing her bed no less! Reg had left town so hastily, he never followed up on what Audrey had done with the display after she removed it from the front of the restaurant. And knowing Shane, it wasn't something that ever occurred to him to ask about.

"Oh, actually, it's really too much of a mess right now." Audrey tried to shove Shane aside and get the door closed behind them as quickly as possible. "Why don't you come back tomorrow after Housekeeping has been through?"

"I don't care about a mess." He pushed on the door as Audrey tried to pull on the door handle.

"I'd rather you didn't," she protested with a tug.

"What's the big deal?" His strength made this a losing battle for her.

"Personal items, okay?" Her eyes defied him. And won.

He lifted his palms in surrender. "Alright, Sugar. Let's go. I've got to stop by Feed U first."

Audrey bit her lip in relief.

Shane drove them to the parking lot at the warehouse kitchen and they went in. Teen helper Santiago was the only one inside.

Santiago gave Shane his four-part handshake. When he turned to Audrey to do the same, she fumbled less than she had when they met the first time. She remembered the other day here, the guileless faces of the young children with their salad and their bread dough, gazing up at Shane as if he was a superhero. If only she'd had a superhero to look up to when she was a kid.

"What are you cooking?" Shane asked Santiago.

"Me and my cousins are going to try to make tamales like our great-grandma used to do."

Audrey noticed the bags of groceries on the counter.

"Okay, you know I can't let you cook without an adult here. You'll wait until Lois comes?"

"Yeah, man, no problem."

"And you'll lock everything down if she wants to leave and you stay to clean up?"

"Yeah, no problem. Thanks."

"Alright. Have fun." Shane handed him the keys.

"Man, it's good to see you," Tino said as he pulled Shane in for a bear hug.

"Been too long," Loke followed with a clinch for his old kitchen mate.

"Audrey, I want you to meet Tino and Loke." Shane introduced her to his two friends who were also cooking in Las Vegas. "The three of us go all the way back to apprenticing in Paris with Pierre."

Shane had been in and out of Vegas for months as he readied the restaurant but had made excuses to avoid hanging out with these guys. They were from a different time in his life. When he had been full of ideas and dreams.

Funny, but he felt some of those old feelings of hope and possibility coming back now.

Tonight, just like when he went to visit Josefina, he was very happy to have Audrey there with him, seeing these pals from the old days. The way she made him feel seemed to give him courage. Drive him forward. Finally.

"Oh, yeah, we'll never forget Paris," said Loke, a short but solid wall of muscle who hailed from Osaka. He shook Audrey's hand. With a perfect French accent, Loke mimicked their old instructor to a T. "Zee pate a choux muz be creesp ahn hallo."

Tino, a lanky Italian American, and Shane nodded in memory. "You muz slap zee dough aginst zee saucepan," Tino chimed in with his pretty good impersonation. He shook Audrey's hand, as well.

Shane added, "The guy was a major pill, but darn if we didn't learn how to make profiteroles in our sleep."

"I'm hungry. Let's eat," Tino urged.

The four left the entrance where they had met and strutted through the casino floor at the MGM Grand. The night was hopping with its herds of people who had fled their normal lives to come to the mirage that was Las Vegas.

The lights and sounds of the slot machines permeated the casino. Clangs signifying jackpots came from every direction even though, in reality, it was the casinos that gained win after win.

Cocktail waitresses in skimpy costumes hoisted trays of drinks while maneuvering through the rows of gaming tables. Blackjack, roulette and craps games were all in play. High rollers puffed on cigars while women who'd had too much cosmetic surgery sat beside them, some dragging on cigarettes in designated smoking areas and others looking around, hoping to be noticed. Poker tournaments and high-stakes games like baccarat were being played in areas partitioned off to the sides of the main gaming floor.

Besides the gamblers, people crossed the casino floor headed in every direction. The masses were from every corner of the earth, comprised of all colors, all ages, all sizes, all socio-economic classes.

Tourists in sneakers snapped photos. Older people walked slowly or used motor scooters or wheelchairs. Travel group chaperones pointed out casino features in several languages.

Groups of people in their twenties moved in

packs this way or that. Many held cocktails. Among them, all of the young women wore a uniform of little dresses cut way up to there and sky-high heels. Of the men who accompanied them, some wore dress shirts and slacks while others looked incongruous with their dates in T-shirts and baseball hats, and some even in sports shorts.

Audrey and her curves looked hotter than any other woman around in her fitted black top tucked into a tasteful skirt. That body of hers was a true hourglass shape and Shane was starting to catch himself on far too many occasions imagining what all those inclines and angles might feel like without clothes to cover them. He'd held her during that crazy kissing on top of his car but, even in the throes of that, he'd censored himself from letting his hands wander too much.

The back of his mind lectured the front lobes that good things came to those who waited. Although, really, he shouldn't be waiting to experience her naked flesh because that was not going to happen. Never. Ever.

Nonetheless, when he was with her he was unable to direct his eyes anywhere else.

The end of the enormous casino gave way to the promenade of shops and restaurants. It was here that Loke was cooking at Shinrin, a small plates and sushi bar favored by the younger set as the cocktail menu was longer than the one for the food.

"Look at this place," Audrey said to Shane as they entered the restaurant.

"Vegas, baby." Shane placed his hand on Audrey's back as Loke escorted them in.

Shane remembered how impressed he and Audrey had been at the Big Top nightclub with its high-concept circus design, perfectly implemented. In fact, Shane had lain awake thinking about every tiny detail of that night at the club. It was that night, the magnificence of Big Top mingled with his heady memories of sensually dancing in a frenzy with Audrey that had served to crack his internal shutters open a little bit. Every step that had led him to be able to come up with a new recipe today was connected to Audrey.

The theme of Shinrin was that of a forest.

Miniature fir trees stood in clusters that divided the space into semi-private areas of couches covered in checkered fabric to give them a picnic look. Patrons ate from low tables made of tree trunk slices where communal plates for sharing were served.

Loke gestured for them to take a seat at two small couches facing each other with a table in between. Shane helped Audrey to one and Tino took the other. While they settled in, Loke dashed away and returned with a ceramic flask of sake and four matching cups. "My cohorts are going to bring us some nibbles," he said and sat beside Tino.

"I stayed at your hotel in Key West," Tino said to Audrey as they sipped their rice wine.

"Ooh—" Audrey smiled "—I hope everything was good?"

"Yeah, first class. I like those huge wooden and brass fans in the front lobby."

"Thanks. We had the blades hand carved."

Loke pointed to Shane and asked Audrey, "Where did you get the idea to partner with this pain in the butt in Vegas?"

"We've been in business with the Murphys

for a decade with the Lolly's casual eateries. But when we bought the old Royal Neva here, we knew we needed a big restaurant."

"Reg had been thinking about an expansion to Vegas, anyway. Who wouldn't want to showcase here, where you can pull out all of the stops? When the Girards asked us to consider venturing in, the pieces fit."

Much as he loved these guys, he wasn't going to tell them how much he needed Vegas. Just like he didn't want to acknowledge how much he was beginning to need Audrey.

Tino lifted his sake cup in a toast and the others followed suit. "To the Murphy brothers in Vegas. Long may you reign."

Shane looked over to Audrey, at the smooth cheeks he had enjoyed running his lips across. How cute she was sitting there with one leg crossed over the other, both shapely legs on view.

"Thank you, Emi," Loke said to the pretty waitress who delivered some plates. He pointed to one of them. "Ankimo sushi. Monkfish liver."

Tino and Shane laughed as they battled each other for what they thought was the choicest piece on the plate. Loke lifted one, as well.

Audrey didn't. Shane wasn't surprised but wondered how to handle what food might be arriving, knowing that she wasn't an adventurous eater. He didn't want to embarrass her.

"Unagi." Loke pointed to another plate.

"You'll like that one," Shane said to Audrey, knowing it was cooked eel brushed with a sweet glaze. "Trust me on that."

She lifted a piece on rice and took a tentative bite. And shot a sly smile at him that went straight to his heart. If this was a different world, he might like to spend his life figuring out things he could do for her that would earn him that kind of smile.

Emi delivered more dishes. Loke pointed, "Karaage."

"Fried chicken," Shane translated.

"I want some," Audrey said quickly. In his zeal, Shane reached for a morsel and fed it to Audrey. Then immediately wished he hadn't in front of Tino and Loke.

When Audrey excused herself to the ladies' room, Shane knew he was going to get grilled.

Tino started, "What's going on there?"

"A corporate partnership." Shane put up his palm as if to shut Tino down.

"Uh-huh." Loke bent in to take another piece of unagi. "I'd like to see what Fat Riku in the kitchen would do if I tried to feed him a bite with my fingers."

"I know, I shouldn't have done that." Shane chuckled, still shocked at his own lack of censorship. Although he shouldn't be surprised. Whenever he got anywhere near Audrey's succulent mouth, he didn't do his most prudent thinking.

"Been a long time for you, man," Loke said. "You dated anyone since Melina died?"

"I'm not dating Audrey!"

"I'll tell you," Tino persisted, "the way you hardly take your eyes off of her looks like a different kind of merger to me."

Loke picked up a piece of ankimo and, with fluttering eyelashes and a quivering mouth, fed it to Tino. The two busted out laughing.

Shane flared his nostrils like he was a bull about to charge at them. But then he cracked up, too. It was about time he laughed at himself.

These guys were really fun to be around. He wished he hadn't waited so long to see them.

After dinner, they decided to play some blackjack in the casino. They were able to find a table with four stools available. None of them were planning to gamble big—it was just to have some fun. Bets were placed and the dealer doled out the cards.

"Eighteen, Loke, you're good," Tino said. "Argh, what do I do on fifteen?"

"Hit," Audrey said without missing a beat.

"Ah ha, the lady is a gambler?" Tino raised an eyebrow.

Audrey smiled at Tino.

Then she turned to Shane.

Then Shane fastened his eyes on her.

Then time stood still.

Then the lights and sounds of the casino faded into a foggy distance.

Then talk of Audrey as a gambler had nothing to do with blackjack anymore.

CHAPTER NINE

"Oh, no," Shane exclaimed when he checked his phone while he and Audrey, Tino and Loke were wrapping up their blackjack session at the MGM. He shoved his and Audrey's gambling chips over to Tino, grabbed Audrey by the hand and pulled her up from her seat. "There's a fire at Feed U. We'll talk to you guys later."

Audrey ran to keep up with him as he tugged her across the casino and out to the valet station. "What happened?" she asked as they waited for his car to be retrieved.

"I don't know. Darn it, I missed three calls from Santiago before he texted." And attempts to return the teenager's calls were going unanswered. Shane tabbed to another phone number and explained to Audrey, "Lois.

"She doesn't know anything about it..." He kept Audrey updated as he talked to Lois. "She went home two hours ago. Santiago's family had finished cooking and they were cleaning up when she left."

"Should we call the fire department?"

"We're close by. We'd better go see what's going on."

Shane swung into the driver's seat of the Jeep as one of the valets helped Audrey in. He palmed the guy a tip, gunned the gas pedal and pulled a sharp left to get away from the Strip as quickly as possible.

When they careened into Feed U Santiago and two other teenagers were in the parking lot, trying to get their phones to work.

"What's happening?" Shane charged out of the car and toward them.

"Fire! Our phones aren't working." Santiago was distraught as he cried out. "Two of my cousins are still inside!"

Shane raced over to the door, which was ajar, and he was able to kick it open farther. Once he saw the blaze inside, he turned back to Audrey and yelled, "Call the fire department!"

Putting an arm in front of his face as a shield, Shane entered. Smoke engulfed the kitchen from flames centered around the stove. He remembered that he had a blanket in the back of the Jeep so he stepped back out to call to Audrey, "Bring me the blanket."

She quickly met him at the door and he used the blanket as a cape and hood to protect himself as he went back in.

"What are your cousins' names?" Audrey yelled behind her to Santiago.

"Denise is twelve and Celia is eight."

Audrey joined Shane inside as he was moving toward the fire.

"Go back!" he shouted to her.

"I'll help. Let me under the blanket."

Not wanting to take the time to argue, Shane threw a piece of the blanket over her and they charged forward.

"Denise!" Audrey called out. Flames crackled and visibility was low.

Smoke and ash burned Shane's eyes. He commanded Audrey, "Shield your eyes.

"Celia!" she yelled.

"Denise!"

"Celia!"

Shane and Audrey moved farther toward the flames. Stacks of kitchen towels succumbed to the fire's reach. Boxes of dry goods on another surface were burning to dust.

"Celia!"

"Denise!"

Shane's heart beat double time as more seconds elapsed without a response from the girls. Anxiety nearly overtook him. He looked over to Audrey who, like him, had begun to choke on the smoke. Taking a few steps farther into the raging heat, they heard a rustling from under one of the worktables. And both girls rolled toward them.

Audrey picked up the smaller girl and yelled to Shane to take the larger. He did his best to cloak them all in the blanket and they ran out the door. Once outside, Audrey and Shane placed the girls gently on the ground. Santiago and the other cousins rallied around them. Everyone was covered in smoke and soot.

A fire truck arrived and several firefighters dashed into the building. One met with the group to ask questions. Santiago was able to confirm that there was no one else inside and explained what had happened.

The cooking had gone well. After they had

finished and were cleaning up, Lois went home. Santiago hadn't noticed that one of the younger kids had tossed an apron on the stove where it ignited. The greasy frying pans on the burners made matters worse when one of the other guys tried to douse the fire with water. By the time he could get to the fire extinguisher on the wall, the flames had spread too wide for him to contain the blaze.

Santiago, shaken to the bone, turned to Shane. "I'm so sorry, man."

"Look, all that matters is that everyone is okay." Shane blew out a breath. He laid his hand across his chest while he took in huge gasps of air.

As the paperwork was logged, Shane and Audrey stood in their ruined clothes. They used the blanket as best they could to wipe their blackened and sweat-soaked faces, after which Shane called his insurance company.

After the firefighters finished and Santiago's parents and aunts and uncles had picked up their kids, it was finally quiet at Feed U. Audrey and

Shane were alone in the parking lot, exhausted, filthy and thirsty.

"My apartment isn't far from here. Do you want to go there and get cleaned up?" he asked her, glassy-eyed and stunned.

"Sure." She didn't dawdle to answer.

Shane drove them there quickly and steered the car into his underground garage. They rode the elevator to the nineteenth floor of the modern apartment building. With a swipe of his entry fob, Shane opened the door and let Audrey in.

It was a bachelor pad just as she might have imagined it would be. Minimal man-furniture was contemporary and clean, and did its job of not distracting from the floor-to-ceiling windows, which offered a city view. The tops of the large hotels on the Strip stood triumphant in the background. Closer in, offices and university buildings were a reminder that Las Vegas was a thriving metropolis.

Shane rushed into his dark kitchen and returned with two waters. They popped the caps and both drank their entire bottle in one go.

"There's a half bathroom right there." He

pointed to a door off the dining area. "Or do you want to take a shower in the master bath?"

Audrey gulped even though she'd finished drinking her water. The immediacy of the fire and the danger to the kids had triggered an agitated state and her lungs were still pumping faster than normal. But when she thought about entering Shane's bedroom to get naked in his en-suite shower, her heart thumped at a pace so rapid she was worried it was going to burst through her body and race out the door on its own.

Yet the idea of getting out of the burned clothes and washing her grimy hair and skin sounded too good to pass up, and this was hardly a time to be thinking about her inappropriate attraction to Shane. She decided to brave her hesitation. "A shower would be great."

Flipping on the bedroom lights, Shane showed Audrey in. Picture windows looked out to the same view as in the living room. "Sorry about the mess."

It wasn't much of a mess but she appreciated his awareness. Some clothes were strewn on the floor and over a chair. Magazines, an iPad, stacks of paperwork, empty drinking glasses and a couple of books peppered the night-stands. But the sheets and blankets on the bed looked crisp and clean. She couldn't help taking pause at the idea that she was inches away from Shane's bed.

Bed.

Where things besides sleep sometimes happened. For some people. Not her, but some people.

Handing her fresh towels he retrieved from a closet, Shane let her enter the bathroom and then closed the door.

Audrey tossed her ruined clothes into a corner. The heel was broken on one of her shoes and the leather on both was shredded. She stepped into the all-glass shower and blasted the taps. As hot water cascaded down her body, it turned gray and swirled into the drain. She rinsed until the water ran clear and then used the musky-scented soap and shampoo that sat on a shelf.

As the last whoosh of clean water rolled down her, her body quivered at an involuntary memory of Shane sliding against her on St. Thomas. Would she ever be free of that moment? She thought the other night dancing and writhing against him at Big Top nightclub might have eclipsed that split second in the Caribbean, but it hadn't. Perhaps because that brush in the ocean had come at such a young age, and from someone who had made such a strong impact on her.

Tonight, a decade later and most unpredictably, she and that very same influential person had saved lives together. Saved lives! Perhaps the Las Vegas Fire Department would have arrived in time to free Santiago's cousins Denise and Celia from the burning kitchen. But she and Shane were able to do it themselves. They got the girls to safety without harm.

Another memory that Audrey would live with for the rest of her life was lifting petrified eight-year-old Celia and carrying her out to the parking lot. Celia had clutched her around the neck with all of her might, the child feverishly hot and screaming for help even though she was already in Audrey's arms.

Instinct had told Audrey what to do. In that moment, she'd never felt more protective, reliable and capable. Audrey had held the child as if she were her own.

When Audrey stepped out of the shower to dry herself with the fluffy yellow towels Shane had provided, she had one immediate problem. Looking over to the pile of near-ashes that were her clothes, she had nothing to put on. There was no choice but to ask Shane to borrow something.

"Shane," she called as she opened the bathroom door and stuck her head out. When there was no reply, she yelled louder. "Shane!"

With still no answer, she wrapped one of the towels tightly around her, toed out of the bathroom and across his bedroom.

She found him in the kitchen.

"I'm starved. I thought you might be, too," Shane said over the sputtering bacon he was flipping in the skillet. He popped slices of bread into the nearby toaster.

Only then did he look up and see that Audrey was dressed in nothing more than a towel. The look on his face was almost that of a cartoon character whose eyes literally boinged out of their head attached by springs. Audrey would have giggled except Shane's expression swiftly changed to something darker. His eyes slit. His Adam's apple jumped.

Wet hair draped across her still-dewy shoulders. Her lips parted ever so slightly as their eyes froze for a moment in which what wasn't said was a lot. Sizzles ran up and down her body, mimicking the sound of the bacon.

"I need to borrow something to wear," she rasped.

"You certainly do," he concurred while clearing his throat. "And quick."

He fought a smile trying to break through.

If she were a different person, she might have let the towel drop to the floor then and there. Done something crazy and impulsive that she would have regretted later. But that wasn't her. Was it?

"Top drawer of the dresser." Shane returned her to practicality. "There are T-shirt or sweats. Whatever you think will fit you best." His eyes dropped to her bare legs.

She turned away and returned to his bedroom, somehow a little disappointed in herself.

All of his sweatpants were impossibly long

on her so she settled for a big T-shirt that hung halfway down her thighs. That was greeted with another look-see from Shane that she interpreted as lustful.

As to the matter at hand, Shane laid out a much-appreciated meal of bacon, eggs and toast on square Asian-inspired plates.

"Do you have any jam?" Audrey asked as she took a seat at the dining table.

"Of course. How could I forget, Sugar?"

He fetched her a pot of what looked like homemade jam. "You go ahead and eat. It's my turn for the shower."

As welcome as the food tasted, all of Audrey's attention was alert to the fact that Shane was taking a shower in the next room.

She recalled that this day had started with Shane's success in the restaurant kitchen using his grandma's pots and pans. It then progressed to the casino night with his friends at the MGM before the fire at Feed U. And now to here. It wasn't just the smoke that made her eyes feel heavy.

"My phone battery died. What time is it?" she asked when he returned wearing a pair of sweatpants that rode low on his hips and a white T-shirt that kept nothing of his muscled torso a mystery.

"It's 4:00 a.m."

While Shane ate, they discussed the fire. "We have so many safety checks in place, nothing like that has ever happened in any of our kitchens," he explained.

"And, of course, you have staff who are trained in emergency procedures," she agreed and took a sip of the tea he had prepared. "We had a dryer fire in a laundry room once. Certain oils and products the spa uses can be highly flammable. But it was quickly contained and no one was hurt."

"Kids. I'll chew the heck out of Santiago later, but I wasn't going to say anything tonight when he was scared half to death." Shane chomped on a slice of bacon.

"As well he should have been. I shudder to think what would have happened if we hadn't got there when we did."

"Those little munchkins' faces..." Shane blinked his eyes in distress. "Heartbreaking."

Audrey forked up the last of her eggs. "You like kids, huh?"

"Hmm. Yeah. I guess I do. I like how they just tell it as it is. And they always see the best in things."

"Do you think you'll ever have any of your own?"

Shane filled his cheeks with air like a balloon and then deflated them. "Absolutely not."

Audrey wasn't sure why the space between her shoulder blades tightened.

"I couldn't even be responsible for the safety of a grown woman," Shane said with a frown. "I sure as heck couldn't be trusted with the well-being of a munchkin. Look at tonight. Thank heavens none of them were hurt, but I shouldn't have agreed to let Santiago close up the kitchen."

"Lois was there until she thought they were done."

"Doesn't matter. My kitchen. My problem." He bit into a piece of toast. "What about you? Little Girards in your future?"

She quickly nodded. "No way. I'd have absolutely no idea what to do with a child."

"Why do you always talk about kids as if they were a separate species?"

"Do I?"

"And when I took you to cook with them you seemed so uneasy."

Audrey stuck her knife in the jar of jam and began spreading some on her toast. Tears threatened from behind her eyes. But this was no time to cry. Children's lives had been at stake tonight. There was no room at the moment for self-pity.

Yet she wanted to confide in Shane.

More than wanted to.

Needed to.

"That's how my mother made me feel," she said softly with her focus still on her toast.

"How?"

"You said it exactly right. Like I was a different species." She put the toast down, suddenly not hungry for it. "I guess the apple doesn't fall far from the tree. My mother was uncomfortable around kids. Around me."

"Why do you think that was?"

"She was afraid of me. Because she never understood my needs and didn't believe she was up to the task of parenting."

"Didn't she have anyone around her to help her be a mother? In my big Irish family there were my grandmas and four aunts, and they were all always meddling in each other's parenting."

Audrey shook her head. "She cut herself off from everybody." Her lip trembled. "Depression ran my mom's life. Alcohol and pills were her only friends."

"Where was your dad in all of this?"

"He saw what he wanted to see. He had the hotels to run. His response was to make the hotels my home away from home and my playground. And then to teach me the business. Not a bad way to go, under the circumstances."

Daniel Girard was like a big kid himself. Always optimistic. Assuming the next day would be even better than the last. He probably thought he was sheltering Audrey by letting her grow up around hotel staff who watched over her.

Still, there was nothing to replace a mother's love. The hole in her heart that nothing would ever fill.

Audrey looked out Shane's windows over-looking the city. She mashed her lips, attempting to seal in the emotions that were trying to overflow. She'd said enough.

Shane sensed that she was deep in her own pain. He reached a hand over and put it on top of hers. Her head tilted slightly toward him.

"Alright, two people who think they are completely unsuitable to be parents put themselves in danger to protect some children tonight anyway."

The irony brought a curve to her lips.

Shane shifted his chair closer to her. He moved his thumb across her piece of toast to get a swipe of jam.

"You didn't taste my jam yet, Sugar. Blackberry." He brought his thumb close to her mouth, daring her to lick it.

Which she was unable to resist. The fruit was especially sweet from the pad of his fingertip.

He thumbed another smear of jam and spread it across her bottom lip. "I'd like to try it myself," he said in a low, gravelly voice.

Taking her face in both hands, he pulled her

to him. With the tip of his tongue he flicked the jam from the soft pillow of her lip.

"Mmm," he moaned his approval. The timbre of the sound coursed like an infusion straight through Audrey's veins. She'd give the world just to hear it once more. Shane obliged by again licking her lip and again moaning with pleasure.

One of his hands moved to the back of her head, threading his fingers through her hair. The other hand remained on her face, caressing her cheekbone.

This wasn't supposed to be happening again. Kissing him. The episode on top of his car had arisen spontaneously. The sunset had been beautiful and they were curious. But this time they knew better.

Yet the back of Shane's big hand stroking her cheeks, one then the other, over and over, rendered her utterly powerless to stop him.

He'd enjoyed the jam kiss so much that he spread the purple sweetness on her lips for another. This time his warm tongue made an ever-so-slow circle all the way around her mouth before that sound roiled up from his belly, and then surged through her body. Her lower back arched inward.

In a sudden move, he gathered all of her hair in one hand. With the other, he used a finger to paint a line of jam from behind her ear down to the base of her neck. He made her anticipation build toward the inevitable, leaning over to let his hot breath settle against her tender skin before he gradually licked away his marking.

Then he took her mouth fully, joining it to his. Her lips rose up to him. He kissed her over and over, each meeting delivering more urgency than the one before.

He reached under the table and slid his hand beneath the T-shirt she had borrowed, feeling only bare skin underneath. Audrey gasped. His sure fingers clutched pieces of her. Her thigh. Her hip. All the way up to her waist.

In one fell swoop, he pushed his chair back to lift her into his arms and stood up. Her hands draped around his neck of their own volition, as if they knew they were supposed to go there, knew that was where they belonged.

Fear tried desperately to grip hold of her as he carried her to his bedroom. She shouldn't do this. It would be a mistake. But if she knew it was wrong, why did she have a box of condoms in her purse that she had bought this morning when she stopped at the store for toothpaste?

Shane sat her down on his bed and slid off the thin T-shirt that had concealed her body. He laid her down and began to explore every inch of her. His curious hands were closely followed by his mouth, causing tiny pinpoints of sensation to bring her higher and then higher still. Yet he modulated his pace so that she lifted when he wanted her to, carrying her up slowly. When he let her glide free, she flew into the air on a cloud of ecstasy he never wanted her to come down from. Moments later, her earlier purchase was put to good use as their bodies soared together through the dawn skies, where they crested in each other's arms. Until the sun rose across the desert.

When the bright morning light hit his eyes, Shane rolled over for the remote control atop his nightstand that lowered the blinds on his bedroom windows. He had only slept for a couple of hours. Exhaustion weighed heavy in his bones. Beside him was glorious Audrey. With her spun-sleek hair and her velvety skin and her luxurious flesh reminding him of the exquisite pleasures they had just shared.

He wanted to wake her up with easy kisses down the entire length of her body. His own solid core let him know that's exactly what he ached to do.

Yet his brain told him something else entirely.

As he watched exquisite Audrey take in the gentle breaths of peaceful sleep, Shane's chest thundered with panic and regret.

CHAPTER TEN

CONSTRUCTION WAS NOT yet complete at the back of the hotel, so no one saw Shane drop Audrey off. With her burned and torn clothes now in Shane's trash can, she was suited up in a ridiculous outfit of his belted overcoat and a pair of his flip-flops that were twice the size of her feet. Key card in hand, she hurried to her bungalow and slipped inside.

Cardboard Shane pinged his tongue against his top lip as she entered. A silly grin broke out on her face as she plopped backward down on the bed. She lifted the collar of Shane's coat to find a faint smell of him.

Being wrong had never felt this right. Every inch of her body tingled as she recalled snippets of what they had just shared. His strong body entwined with hers in every possible configuration. Taut muscles presenting firm walls for her bonelessness to wrap around. The hypnotism of his kisses that robbed her mind of any past or any future.

Audrey had only been intimate with a couple of men. Both experiences were a long time ago and nothing like the heights she'd just climbed to with Shane. It shouldn't have come as a surprise to her that he held more passion in the crook of his finger than most of the people she'd ever met in her life had combined. Lying on her bed in his coat, she swooned.

They'd be reuniting in four hours to tape a segment of the cooking special. Two hundred and forty minutes until she would be back together with him. She painstakingly set her phone to alert her every half hour so that the time she had to wait to see him would be broken down into manageable stretches of time.

What?

Had she gone crazy? They got lost in the moment and had sex last night. It had no long-term meaning. They were still only business partners, not open to becoming involved with anyone, and last night was not going to change a thing.

Nevermind that her emotions after the fire

at Feed U had led her to tell him more about what she'd bottled up inside than she'd ever told anyone. And nevermind that they had shared a lovemaking so poignant he had reached down into her and grabbed hold of her very being. Nevermind that in his arms she started to have new insights into something beyond arranged marriages and workaholic companionship.

Reality gnawed. Those were all silly day-dreams. She knew all too well not to confuse them with reality.

But what if?

Audrey dressed for the appointment she had before the taping, a visit with a former Girard employee who was now a wedding coordinator at The Venetian. After kisses on both cheeks, Grace showed Audrey the wedding chapel at the stylish hotel. Grace lifted a slender finger up to her lips to let Audrey know that they should be quiet because a ceremony was taking place.

The bride was a fairy princess in a short-sleeved gown with a sweetheart neckline and a ballroom skirt that must have been constructed with yards upon yards of tulle to create its shape. Her dark skin glowed while her short curly hair was enhanced by a pearly headband attached to her veil. The slim groom stood tall in his traditional tuxedo, the bow tie and cummerbund a sky blue that matched his three groomsmen and the dresses of the three bridesmaids who stood in their designated places. A small group of guests filled the front pews.

Audrey couldn't hear what the officiant was saying to the couple in a muffled voice meant only for them, nor did she need to. The classic scene was profound and pastoral. She blinked repeatedly as a way of keeping tears from spilling down her face.

The way the bride and groom gazed at each other, she doubted they heard a word that was said, either. To each, there was nothing in the room but the other. Immeasurable happiness, pure love and total certainty emanated from both of them. Audrey mused on what plans they may have made and what they were looking forward to in their lives. Hopefully nothing but death would take them from each other and maybe not even that.

Audrey had been completely sure that nothing like that was ever in her future. That would involve trust, and she surely wasn't going to fall for that one again. If you couldn't trust your mother, your own flesh and blood, you surely couldn't count on someone who fundamentally came to you as a stranger. Love could only turn to disappointment and setback.

But when she was with Shane, anything seemed possible. Really, it had been building all along. From watching him cook with the little kids at Feed U to his friendship with Josefina to his warm memories of his own grandmother. With his insistence on perfection in his work. From his willingness to show her his vulnerable side in admitting that he hadn't loved his wife. And from the sunset kisses that were more than just physical attraction. Kissing him was an act of two spirits meeting. And what passed between them in his bed carried stories for all the ages.

Here she was in a predicament she was hardly expecting. Reg had fallen for someone else and her safety net had been pulled out from beneath her. Someone with lesser moral standards might have gone through with the arranged marriage and continued to see his true love at the same time. But Reg was a fair enough man not to allow any deception and had come forward straight away. Reg hadn't foreseen this, and Audrey did wish him well.

After that change of track, she'd returned all of her focus to her work. Which, bizarrely, entailed being at Shane's side much of the time. And now, for the good of all, not the least of whom was Shane himself, it seemed that he had been able to reclaim his magic.

Little could Audrey have known that along the way she'd find some of her own.

Shane was adamant that he'd never be in another relationship. Audrey herself had been decided, too. She still clutched a hurt that would never stop bleeding.

So why was it that now she wanted more than anything in the world to wear a white dress and hear Shane say words like *for better or for worse* and *as long as we both shall live*? Words that caused a couple to stare at one another like the pair she watched right now in the chapel. In each other's eyes, and in the promises they spoke, the past could be healed and the future was limitless. Yes, there would be disappointments and mistakes and tears, but they would weather the lows and embrace the highs. Together.

She wanted that with Shane.

More than anything she'd ever wanted in this world.

What was he feeling after last night? Had the floodgates been opened for him, too? He was cooking again. More important still, he was conceiving again, tapping into that divinity that worked through him to create. Had he crossed over? Were they ready for each other?

Grace whispered to snap her out of her turmoil, "Audrey!"

She took in the panorama of the chapel and returned to earth. "Sorry, lost in thought."

Graced smiled. "What's his name?"

Later in Grace's office over cappuccinos they discussed event planning in Vegas. From there, Audrey returned to Hotel Girard and popped into her dad's office.

"'Yummy chef Shane Murphy was spotted on the Strip again last night with delicious hotelier Audrey Girard and a couple of other friends,'" Daniel read from his phone. "'While they may have been hooting and hollering at the black-jack table, it looked like these two were ready to place a bet on each other.'"

"Dad, you wouldn't believe what happened last night after that," she exclaimed. And proceeded to tell him all about the fire. And nothing at all about the fireworks.

"Hi." Audrey offered Shane a flirty smile when he came up to the swanky rooftop pool for the TV taping.

She bit her lower lip in order not to faint at the sight of him in the outfit she had worked through with the stylist. He'd wear his cook's coat for a later shoot in the restaurant and she was even considering having him in a tuxedo while he talked about food during a cocktail party segment. She had the feeling Shane would look good wearing anything. Last night, he looked mighty good wearing nothing. But for the rooftop it was white jeans, white button-down shirt, tan shoes and belt, and his own aviator sunglasses. Casual elegance that was pure crazy, in a great way, with his wild long curls and nicely groomed beard stubble.

Audrey's spine vibrated as her brain re-played that stubble awakening every part of her it touched last night. Those scratchy hairs demanded her full attention. And received it without a fight.

"Hi," he clipped in a tight voice and looked away. No doubt he was dreading this taping. At the height of his stardom a few years ago, he was on talk shows presenting cooking demon-strations left and right, so he knew how it was done. Maybe the process had probably become unfamiliar to him now.

Or perhaps he was tired today. They surely hadn't used his bed for much sleeping.

What sleeping they did do may have been as profound to her as the lovemaking. It had been years since she'd shared a bed with anything but a pillow.

Busy career gal, husbandless and childless, gives her all to the family legacy.

Nothing wrong with that. It was what she'd thought she'd wanted.

Now, suddenly, she coveted more. She wanted the whole shebang. To lie every night in a big bed with Shane's long arms around her. To yawn during sleepy-time chitchat about their days, the successes, the failures. And she wanted to stand beside him as together they showered little Girard-Murphys with all the love she had to give, which lately had grown to infinitely more than she thought she had. She wanted to work hard, play hard, love hard.

Everything her dad told her she might feel some day was right. Because of Shane. She'd never have opened up to anyone like she did with him. Maybe Josefina had been right when she said that tragedy would bind them together. Could it be what would set them free, as well?

The TV crew had created a small set for Shane to cook from on the bridge between the swimming pools. Everything was in its place. Just as Audrey had visualized it. On the chic rooftop pool area of Hotel Girard with the Las Vegas Strip visible in the background, this opening segment of the TV special would create instant appeal for the property and its location. It was the Vegas fantasy come true. Stylish fun in the sun, great food and drink, gaming and entertainment at every turn.

"This is going to look fabulous on camera,"

she said as she ushered Shane to his spot at the makeshift kitchen. "Everything okay?"

"Are we ready?" Phil, the director, called over.

"Just dandy," Shane snapped at Audrey, taking her back a little. She knew he'd rather be almost anywhere else but he could be a bit more pleasant. Wasn't the memory of last night enough to put him in a good mood?

"Let's try a take, Shane," Phil instructed. Audrey moved to the side of the bridge to be out of the shot. "Places, please. And we go in five, four, three, two, one, cue Shane."

Shane turned on his electric smile. "Shane Murphy here on the rooftop of the Hotel Girard Las Vegas, site of my newest Shane's Table restaurant…" He continued to read from the teleprompter and kept on his camera face for a couple of minutes before asking for a break.

"All good, Shane?" Phil asked. "You look great."

"Delightful." Shane shot the answer at Audrey in a voice that suggested he was anything but.

Don't take it personally, she coached herself.

"I'm sorry we're taking up your time," Audrey said to him by way of apology because he seemed so uncomfortable. Although, obviously, all of this was meant to benefit both of their interests. This morning he had said that he was anxious to try out a couple of recipe ideas so, she reasoned, maybe he was impatient because he would rather be in his kitchen. Where his heart was. In his think tank. His kingdom. Ultimately, the place where he felt at home.

If he didn't want to be shooting the show right now, she wished with all of her might that they weren't. But they had a job to do.

"Picking up where we left off," Phil called, "in three, two, one."

Shane flipped on his dazzle switch again. "We're going to do a refreshing first course for a poolside gathering. Watermelon gazpacho. Gazpacho refers to a cold, raw soup and there are hundreds of different preparations. It's classic to use a tomato base, and we're going to put a Mediterranean spin on it with watermelon and a finish of feta cheese. You'll be surprised how great the pairing of the acid in the tomato plays against the supersweet melon."

Audrey watched Shane do his thing as he

began explaining the ingredients and method. The way he managed to be authoritative but warm and friendly at the same time filled her with admiration. Were this formidable and complex man to be hers, she'd treasure every facet of him because they added up to who he was. She'd have to learn to back off when he wanted to be left alone. Not to read into it a rejection of her. Not everyone was her mother.

"Gazpacho is thought to have originated in Andalusia," Shane continued, the absolute professional. "Some recipes pulverize a piece of bread and blend that in to create a thickness that is hard to achieve in an uncooked soup. It was probably the ancient Romans who brought that concept over to Spain."

Shane completed the gazpacho, showing his would-be audience a variety of attractive serving suggestions. He poured the soup into small clear glasses, which he arranged on a wooden tray. In heavy blue margarita glasses with stems, the mixture resembled a refreshing cocktail. And ladled into small porcelain bowls with long slices of green bell peppers as a garnish, the gazpacho looked more traditional.

Concluding, he said to the camera, "We'll see you over at the restaurant where we're doing tacos on the patio."

"And…cut." Phil ended the session.

Audrey rushed onto the bridge. "Perfect. It couldn't have gone better."

"Yep, it was a good segment." Shane didn't look at her but busied himself stacking up some plates.

Actually, were they to be together, she was going to need some practice weathering his moods. At the moment, she couldn't understand why he didn't seem to want her near. Was it because of the taping? Something he'd probably rather not have been doing? But both families had agreed this kind of big push was needed to get the hotel and restaurant off to a successful start. He must have known that the segment was flawless and that he'd done his duty.

When people saw this cooking special on TV, Audrey was sure the seed would be planted in their minds that, when in Vegas, a stop at Shane's Table at the Hotel Girard would be an experience in modern fine dining they wouldn't want to miss.

"How was it—" she decided to test the waters "—being in front of the cameras again? I know it's been a long time for you."

"It was fun. I actually enjoyed it." Shane answered her yet kept his eyes on the workspace in front of him.

"Shane?" Audrey couldn't stand him not looking at her.

Without a word, he roped one arm around her waist and brought her close. He took hold of her hair with the other hand and kissed her mouth violently. She responded to his force and met his power as best she could.

After kissing him on the hood of his car and then a thousand ways last night, she knew his kisses. This one was different. It was defiant. It was contemptuous. There was fury in it.

Despite how much she had been trying to convince herself that Shane was merely out of his element in front of the cameras, she had to admit that what was bothering him had something to do with her.

After a long evening of solitary work in the empty kitchen, Shane amped his music even louder to keep him company while he cleaned up. He was pleased with his progress tonight. The tlayudas would fit well in the antojitos, snacks, section of the cookbook. Wanting to offer a vegetarian option, he hadn't yet found the perfect substitute for the chewy tasajo beef. Maybe shiitake mushrooms?

As he dunked some sponges into hot soapy water and began scouring the worktables, the thought he had pushed away for the last few hours fought for its rightful place. The five-foot two-inch intrusion would wait no longer. He'd used the lengthy cooking session to avoid concentrating on one thing. One "she" thing. Audrey.

That kiss earlier at the rooftop pool had almost done him in, and from it he came running into the kitchen to hide and retreat.

All of his emotions had built up. At first, he'd tried to keep Audrey at arm's distance and just get through the taping. He'd said he would do the TV show and he needed to give it all he had. Which he did. But Audrey kept coming closer until he'd snapped and kissed her with a power he didn't like. Because it was a mixture of love and rage. Fortunately, the crew had been taking a break so no one saw him lose his restraint.

Darn her. For having those honey-colored eyes. For letting him trace jam down her neck and taste her sweetness mixed with the fruit. For being alive and responsive in his bed.

For making him abandon all the vows he took after Melina's death.

That he was never again going to care about a woman. Definitely not going to feel accountable to her. He'd loused that up in the most crucial way and he couldn't put someone in that kind of danger again. For their own safety.

His phone vibrated in his pocket. Why did he have a fleeting thrill that it might be Audrey?

It was Reg.

"Hey, did you talk to that guy Eli about the executive chef position? I video called him. He might be alright." Shane and his departing executive chef Lee had made dozens of calls to try to find a replacement. One prospect emerged, a friend of a friend who had the appropriate past experience.

"We're going to give him a try. Lee renegotiated his new deal to stay with us for a couple of weeks longer and train him."

"Thank goodness. What else?"

"It was Hammett who was stealing from us." A barback who had been with them less than a year.

"Jeez." Shane crooked the phone between his ear and shoulder so that he could continue his cleanup.

"We fired him."

"Man, you never know about people. How's it going with Brittany?"

"Risk and potential," Shane's ever-logical brother answered. "What's new there?"

Shane wanted to tell Reg something about Audrey. But his throat blocked. He felt excruciating remorse at having made love with her last night. That was a line that was profoundly unfair to cross. He knew she hadn't been physical with anyone in a long time. Maybe as long as it had been for him, maybe even longer. But they had no business doing that.

They had been partly spurred on by the fire at Feed U, all the adrenaline from the drama and danger surging through them. But he was wrong to have allowed himself to get swept up by emotion. Something he did far too often around Audrey. Acting without thinking was always a mistake. He could hardly face her today.

Audrey had been through her own personal wringer with a mother who hadn't wanted her. Audrey shouldn't take any kind of chance on him, he was not a safe wager. She'd have better odds at the casino.

He could only hurt her. He would hurt her. He probably already had.

"We're on schedule out here." Shane could at least report that much to Reg. "I'll see you soon, bro."

Shane quickly ended the call, too restless to talk. He scrubbed the kitchen from top to bottom until it glistened but still couldn't work out his growing discomfort.

Glad he kept a pair of swim trunks in his desk, he decided to hit the employee pool for a late-night swim to try to blow off his anxiety.

He heard splashing as he entered the pool area. Sure enough, there was Audrey, her petite length gliding from one end of the water to the other.

What an amazing creature she was, gliding through the pool. He thought of the fire. How sure and brave she was, marching into the flames if it meant saving the lives of those two children. It was moments like that in life that showed what a person was truly made of.

She proved how much she could care. And she should have that kind of care in return. Even though it wasn't something she was open to receiving, it was something he could never give. Not now. Not ever.

Tempted to leave unnoticed, he decided to confront her. She was entitled to the truth. He dove in and matched his laps to hers so that they reached the end of the pool at the same time.

"What is it with us?" Audrey half smiled. "We're in some kind of sync."

They both noticed a flash of light coming from behind the fence that enclosed the pool area.

"I need to say something, and I'm just going to come right out and say it." Shane commanded her to look him in the eye.

Her eyes opened wide, making Shane want to

cower from the words he was about to speak. But he pressed on.

"I don't take sex casually and I'm guessing you don't, either."

She bit her plump bottom lip.

"But what happened between us was a one-off. A mistake."

Was it the pool water, or did her eyes mist with tears? He knew that he'd make her cry at some point. Best, he thought, sooner rather than later.

She whispered, "I see."

"I can't afford to have anything like that happen ever again."

"You can't afford it?"

"I can't take the chance."

"What chance?"

"That I'll hurt you."

"Shouldn't that be my decision, not yours?"

They both turned to follow the distracting light that flashed above the top of the fence again.

"Please let me finish." Shane gritted his teeth. "I can't let anything develop between us. Maybe if I were a different man. But I'm not. You already mean too much to me, Audrey. My heart can't take it."

"But…"

Whatever she was going to say would be too painful, so he covered her mouth with a kiss. It would be the last one. With his kiss, he gave her all he had inside so he'd always know that deep in her heart, she would remember this moment. It was a kiss that would have to last a lifetime.

There was no question that it would for him. Audrey, Audrey. In such a short time, she'd changed him forever. Brought him back to life, as a matter of fact. Through her, he'd reached up and clutched a bit of hope above the rubble he was buried under. Through her, he believed in himself again.

And only without her could he continue.

When you really love something, you have to let it go. Wasn't that how the saying went? He loved her so much that he had to protect her from him, from what he was, and wasn't, capable or deserving of. As much as it would damage both of them, he had to do what was in her best interest. He didn't merit something as precious as her heart.

He broke from their last kiss and said with finality. "I can finish the cookbook on my own. Because I can't be that close to you. I can't have you spending time in my kitchen. Business partners is all we're meant to be."

Tears streamed down Audrey's face.

"Shane! Audrey!" A voice came over the fence. Their eyes darted toward it. A paparazzo popped up and began flashing his camera at them again and again.

CHAPTER ELEVEN

*Hotel Heiress Can't Choose Between
Restaurant Brothers!*

THAT WAS THE caption above the two photos
that were released to every gossip site on earth.
In one photo, taken last night Shane and Audrey were caught kissing in the employee pool
under the moonlight. The second photo was of
Reg and Audrey posed in the wedding pavilion two weeks ago. When Audrey was wearing that flowered dress she hated. They were
supposed to be taking engagement photos just
for practice. Before Reg changed the plan and
returned to New York.

Audrey stood in her dad's office and shook
her head back and forth. "We saw the camera
flashes last night."

Daniel sat at his desk while Shane leaned back
in his chair, leg spread apart, eyes downcast.

Reg joined them via Skype. "I can't imagine how those first photos of you and me were leaked," he said to Audrey.

"One of the photographer's crew," Daniel said. "Anyone who had access to the photographer's files. Or maybe the guy himself."

"I'll call our lawyer," Reg added, "Although that doesn't help us figure out what to do now."

"Nothing," Audrey said definitively. "We do nothing. Just let it blow over. There will be a different hot story by the next news cycle in a few hours."

Shane gave her half of a smile and then looked back down to the floor.

After the paparazzo had startled them in the pool last night, Shane yelled at the guy. He and Audrey stood dripping wet poolside. She was reeling both from the unexpected intrusion of the photographer, and from Shane's declaration that he no longer wanted her help. That he wouldn't pursue anything personal with her. Which, of course, stung worse than any of the other blows.

After Shane chased the pap away, Audrey did her best to hide the heartbreak that speared through her at his statement of finality. She mumbled a quick good-night and retreated to her bungalow.

Even though they had shared so much together already, he was very clear. He no longer wanted her involved in his life.

He'd made breakthroughs in his cooking. She didn't know if she'd really had anything to do with that other than providing a sounding board. But something seemed to have clicked and he was moving forward at last.

It hadn't been just one-sided. Night after night, she told him everything about her day. Every work challenge she faced or decision she had to make. It gave her focus and clarity to share all of her thoughts. She was doing her best work in years.

Granted, it was a Shane Murphy made out of cardboard she divulged her thoughts to, but without the effect the real Shane had on her, it wouldn't have meant anything.

Which is why she tried to ignore her four-hundred-pound heart and flushed neck as they held this meeting to discuss damage control about the photos. Everything was happening too fast—she really hadn't had a chance to understand or process her disappointment. They were in business together so avoiding Shane wasn't an option, although it's the one she would have chosen if she could have.

Once the meeting was over and Shane left Daniel's office, Audrey sank into a chair by the window. Her dad could tell she was upset and joined her in the chair at her side. They looked out to the action on the Strip. Even during the day, plenty of revelers had drinks in their hands and, probably empty pockets too.

She spotted a group of young women all wearing bridal veils that were attached to red headbands with cat ears. They giggled their way down the boulevard. Must have been an all-night bachelorette party.

Las Vegas, real and fake. The Eiffel Tower. New York skyline. Roman statue. Medieval castle. Ancient pyramid. Shane and Audrey.

Audrey told Daniel that Shane had excused her from her duties. She hadn't spoken to her dad about what had passed between them on a personal level. Since nothing was going to come of it, she saw no reason to now.

Yet he guessed at it. "You have feelings for Shane."

"Never." She pressed her lips together.

"Daughter," Daniel said, reaching over to take Audrey's hand. "I know you had it rough growing up. I was consumed with running the hotels but I wasn't blind. Your mother was a very unusual woman."

"That's one way of putting it."

"I did my best to compensate but I know that for a daughter there's no substitute for a mother. In her own way, though, she did love you. When I'd see her late in the evening after you'd gone to sleep, she'd tell me all about your accomplishments at school."

"After she'd heard about them from the nanny?" A tear slipped from Audrey's eye.

"Yes, but there was pride in her eyes as she listed your achievements."

"Wish I'd been allowed to see that." At least five more tears leaked out.

"Audrey, you're twenty-eight. You have to open some doors and let love in. Set the past to the side. Move forward."

She clutched her father's hand as dozens of

fresh tears dropped down her cheeks. He'd never know that she had opened the door a sliver, only to have it slammed shut in her face.

The rest of Audrey's day was another blur of meetings and decisions. She went out to a local golf course to work on some incentives the hotel would offer. A limo would pick guests up at the Girard where they'd be sent off with a boxed breakfast and hot coffee. At the golf course, they'd have a desirable early-morning tee time before the sun got too blistering. A brunch with mimosas at the eighteenth hole would cap off the morning. Upon returning to the hotel, guests would be welcomed back with a basket full of after-sun products and icy packs for aching muscles plus a nice assortment of fruit, nuts and green juices for the afternoon. All well thought out. An impeccable Girard promotion. The kind of thing Audrey took the most pride in.

Audrey's joke of a dinner was comprised of hummus and pita plus loads of cookies leftover from an earlier meeting with Housekeeping when they discussed press releases about the hotel's energy efficient laundry practices. Afterward, Audrey was restless. She paced her empty bungalow, for the first time not wanting to even look in cardboard Shane's direction. It occurred to her to go out.

It being Vegas, she could participate in any of a hundred different activities. She might see an elaborate show. Or a comedian or a piano-lounge singer. While away some time placing bets on a low-stakes slot machine at one of the big casinos. Drive off the Strip to go to a shopping mall or neighborhood restaurant and spend the evening like a resident Las Vegan.

But none of those options sounded good to her. Unable to inspire herself for anything unfamiliar, she changed into her bathing suit, threw on a cover-up and went to the employee pool.

The sky was especially black. Audrey inched into the pool and then pushed off to begin her methodical laps. She thought of how many laps she had swum in her lifetime. How much she enjoyed the feeling of herself buoyant and fast through the water. Here she often did her best thinking.

Shane. Shane was her best thinking. No one could have planned the unlikely sequence of events that had played out here in Vegas. That once Reg was out the door, her feelings for Shane would creep in the window. The idea of an arranged companionship was usurped by a love so real it decimated all of the pillars Audrey had built and surrounded herself with. Like an innocent ape, one man demolished her blockades with the loping sweep of his mighty arm. And then ran away into the jungle.

Shane had made her fall in love with him. Yet he didn't love her in return. Could there be a more ironic twist of fate in this city of chance?

Audrey swam, kicking off from turns, using measured strokes, taking rhythmic breaths. Back and forth, shallow end of the pool to the deep and then to the shallow again. Was she wishing through every second of it that Shane would appear at the pool like he had every time she'd been swimming since she arrived in Vegas? To tell her he couldn't live without her and everything he had said to her was a mistake? Absolutely.

With every lap, she looked over to check if the gate was opening.

He never came.

Two weeks later...

"Shane, can we get some shots with you and Reg?" one of the invited guests at the press brunch called out.

As he had been for the past two hours, Shane continued to make the rounds at the rooftop event. Reg was flagged over and the two Murphys put on their glittering restaurant brothers act as the photos were snapped. Rail-thin and short-haired, Brittany watched from the sidelines, clearly proud of her man. Reg had on a smart suit, uncharacteristically without a tie to be appropriate for the poolside. Shane wore his chef's coat with black jeans.

"Get the cookbook," Reg, ever practical, instructed as he blotted under his nose with a napkin.

Shane reached for the mock-up he had placed on the stool beside him. *Shane's Table at Home* bore its cover art of him smiling up from the salad he tossed in a big wooden bowl. Pieces of lettuce were miraculously caught in flight. Shane had no idea how a shot like that was achieved. He and Reg had reviewed at least a hundred photos of him for the cover, until they found one that best upheld Shane's brand of rock 'n' roll meets world-class chef.

As he and Reg and the cookbook posed, out of the corner of his eye Shane spotted Audrey with a small circle of interested people surrounding her. Holding up a spa product or something, she seemed to be promoting it to her attentive audience.

His belly contracted at the sight of her, as spectacular as the late-morning sun. If there was ever an electrical outage, her smile could power the Strip.

She looked *brunchalicious* in white slacks, which he could tell were long enough to conceal the very high heels that she favored because she liked to look taller than her petite, yet perfect, height. A gold blouse that crossed in front flattered her marvelous femininity. And her shiny hair in loose waves was that kind of effortless look that probably took a lot of effort.

Sugar.

Indeed.

Over the past two weeks, not an hour had gone by that her stunning face hadn't popped its way

front and center into Shane's mind. He'd felt
certain that he couldn't pursue anything with
her, not the completion of the cookbook nor
what had passed between them personally. That
when you loved something, you had to protect it
even if that meant shielding it from yourself. If
it meant denying himself the one thing he realized he most wanted, so be it. He'd sworn he'd
never again be a hindrance to someone's well-
being, he just couldn't risk having the power to
hurt Audrey. The woman he loved.

The woman he loved.

The past two weeks had been busy from
morning to night but Shane had still found time
to agonize about Audrey and what he was turning his back on. It didn't help that he was involved with her in this business venture that
was vitally important to both of their families.
Normally, if you decided against a relationship,
you could simply walk away and not have to see
that person again.

In the months that turned to years after Melina's death, he'd been asleep in his own trauma.
Audrey had woken him up, spun his wheels in

a new direction. He'd always be grateful to her for that after years of stalling out.

He glanced over and saw his parents, Connor and Tara, talking to Daniel. They had flown in for the opening. He'd had dinner and a heart-to-heart talk with them last night. They knew the next move he'd decided on.

Always one for extremes, in the last two weeks Shane had done nothing but work. Locking himself in the kitchen from dawn to midnight, he focused solely on creating new recipes for the cookbook. He was forced to dig lower into his own well of inventiveness, his knowledge of flavors and of technique. He'd researched foods native to the area, something he always enjoyed. He'd driven to off-the-beaten-track ethnic grocery stores and farmers' markets. In the past two weeks, he'd come up with some of the greatest recipes of his career.

He looked over to the reason. Of course it was because of her. She had reintroduced him to himself.

"Come over here and take a few shots for *Vegas Food and Wine*." Reg guided his brother to do another smile show.

They invited their new manager Enrique over for photos. Shane couldn't have readied the restaurant for opening without his competent service. Rachel in LA had trained him well. After a handshake, Enrique returned to supervising the brunch buffet.

"Mom, Dad, Daniel, can we do some shots?" Shane rounded them up. He beckoned with his hand to the woman he loved who had been watching the grouping. "Audrey, join us please."

After a glance down to the ground, she strode over, shook Brittany's hand on the sidelines and then took her place next to her dad for the photo.

Shane had seen precious little of Audrey in person for the past two weeks. Which was probably for the best, since any time he smelled her perfume or was in proximity of her warm skin, he'd had to rein himself in from breaking his resolve.

After the photo, Shane moved toward the other end of the pool for some hellos. His feet stepped forward but his eyes were glued on Audrey as she shook hands and charmed another grouping of people. The woman he loved in her native habitat, being fabulous at her job.

The woman he loved.

She'd obviously kept her distance from him, as well, these past weeks as email became her preferred method to notify him of business matters. And by including Daniel and Reg in all correspondence, she further professionalized their communications.

Shane had completed the TV show, working through four other segments with Phil. Audrey came by each set to nod her approval but didn't stay for the tapings.

The woman he loved.

Yesterday, Shane had made up his mind. Once and for all. What he carried in his pocket was proof.

The cookbook, the TV show, the restaurants. As important as they were, he'd finally learned what he needed. What mattered the most.

Shane made nice with another cluster of guests enjoying the coffee bar but scanned the pool area until he located Daniel. When he could break away, Shane moved toward him.

As soon as he could budge Daniel away from the woman who was talking his ear off, Shane pulled him over to a quiet area against the rail-

ing overlooking the Strip and asked him the
question that had been bubbling up inside him
and could no longer be contained.

Shane caught Audrey observing them as they
talked.

When Shane took a break from another round
of schmoozing, he found Audrey who had also
paused for a glass of water. "I need to speak
with you in private," Shane whispered in her
ear.

The game face she'd worn through the entire
brunch disappeared.

"I don't think that's a good idea," she eked
out in a constricted voice.

As she started to walk away, Shane reached
out and took hold of her arm. He'd made a mistake two weeks ago. He wasn't going to make
another.

Her body winced at his touch and she froze.
Then turned to face him.

"Let's go out to the desert to watch the sunset after everything wraps up today," he said.
"Like we did that day we went to see Josefina."

That sunset when they'd sat on the hood of his

car and kissed and kissed together until darkness blanketed the mountains.

"I won't, Shane. You said your piece two weeks ago. I can't. You can't."

"I was wrong." His hand slid up her arm.

"You weren't wrong. You know yourself. Just like I know myself."

"Come to the desert with me."

"Shane, let me go. People are going to start to talk," she surveyed the crowd. "After all the photos and the gossip."

"We're business partners, people are going to see us together. Come out with me later."

"No," she insisted. But as his mouth cracked into a tiny smile, so did hers.

His spirit rose up and across every inch his body, cloaking him in a tingling aura of anticipation. That little hint of a smile told him everything he needed to know for the moment. "Audrey!" A voice from the other side of the rooftop called her. She looked over.

"I have to go."

"Say you'll take a drive with me, Sugar."

"Don't call me that."

"Say it."

"No."

"Say it." His smile grew wider. Despite how much he wanted to, he knew he couldn't kiss her now in front of all of these people. But that was sure as heck what he was going to do later. For starters.

"Okay!"

"Okay." He beamed. "I'll come for you at your bungalow."

"You're nuts, you know?"

"But that's what you love about me, isn't it?"

"I don't lo—" She didn't finish what she was saying but scrunched her face in an adorable way and hurried away.

His heart beat triple fast as he watched her go.

When the day was finally done, Shane couldn't believe what he was about to make happen. But he prickled with excitement as he pulled out his phone. *"¿Como estas, amiga?"* he greeted his old friend.

After the call, the spring in his step hurried him to Audrey's bungalow.

"Oops, not quite ready," Audrey said by way of a hello as she opened the door.

Shane leaned in on the door and it opened

farther. He presented the bag he had prepared earlier. "I made you a zucchini lemon basil loaf. Notice how I put vegetables into cake? Can I come in?"

"Of course," she answered over her shoulder but then remembered something. "Oh, I mean, um, can you just wait outside? I'll just be one second."

"Huh?" he asked, having already entered and closed the door behind him. And then he saw the last thing he'd ever expect to see in her bungalow.

Him.

The cardboard cutout of him that Reg had ordered a month ago stood facing Audrey's bed. He'd hated the darn thing but Reg had insisted on putting it up in front of the restaurant. He hadn't seen it since, but with everything that had been going on, he hadn't remembered to ask Reg about its whereabouts.

What on earth was it doing in Audrey's room? Partially, he saw, it was being used for practical purposes. While he stood brooding and serious in his chef's coat, bandanna across his forehead and holding his knife like he meant business, now he also wore Audrey's floppy sunhat on top of his cardboard head. Several necklaces were roped around his neck. A purse with a long strap was balanced on one shoulder. Another two purses hung from the other one. And a few scarfs were tied around his waist.

Audrey's mouth dropped open in shock when she headed toward him and saw him inspecting the cutout.

"And you said *I* was nuts?"

"I can explain."

"Uh-huh, Sugar." He grinned. "You can tell me all about it in the car."

As Shane ushered Audrey into the Jeep, she knew her cheeks were pink from the embarrassment of his discovering the cardboard cutout.

"It was the first day I was here and I meant to bring it to my room just to get it out of the view of the public because I hated it so much," Audrey yammered nervously as Shane cut through side streets until he got them out on the open road. "And then Reg left and I kind of forgot it was there."

Shane glanced sideways at her with hitched eyebrows.

"I mean, before I knew it, it became part of the decor," she continued.

"I like that I've gotten to see you naked every night since you've been here." He smiled but straightened his focus to the road.

She wasn't about to tell him that it wasn't just her nude body but her naked soul that the cutout had been seeing every night. That the cardboard had become her best friend. She relied on it for feedback and for counsel; in fact, it had become her closest confidante. It never judged her, always had a sense of humor and was fiercely on her side. That cutout was good people.

Ten minutes ago, she was trying to get the cutout to talk her out of going on this ride with Shane. After all that had transpired, going out to the spot where they had shared life-altering kisses hardly seemed like a good idea.

Yet she couldn't resist. There wasn't anything she'd rather be doing after a hectic day of overseeing an important event and being *on* with everyone she encountered than driving out of

ANDREA BOLTER

the city to the tranquility of the mountains. With Shane.

Doing anything. With Shane.

"What were you and my dad talking about at the party?" she asked him.

He hesitated, started to say something but then pulled it back. "Just a question I needed to ask him."

"About what?"

He didn't answer.

She loved how once they left the boundaries of the city center, Nevada became vast and unknowable. It was land that held the promise of the West, of exploration and of opportunity. Something in her knew it was important to take this drive with Shane, although she couldn't put her finger on why. Maybe it was for closure. To get them to the next phase they needed to reach in order to work together.

Silence fell upon them for a few minutes. Shane didn't turn up the music as he usually did.

At the most unexpected moment, without taking his eyes off the road, he stated simply, "I love you."

A flush rose across her neck. Her throat parched. A dry murmur pushed through. "I love you, too."

Her eyes welled with tears. Her heart sputtered rather than beat. Welcome to love.

With one hand adequate to maneuver the steering wheel, Shane rested his other on Audrey's thigh. He squeezed it gently and then left his palm there.

For the moment, they were unable to look at each other, and both watched intently as that familiar purple began to descend over the orange and yellow shades of the setting sun.

Everything that had happened between them paraded across Audrey's mind like a slideshow.

"You couldn't have known Melina was going to get into an accident," she said after thinking about it for a long time.

"I'd upset her."

"She was a grown woman. Who should have known better than to drive in unsafe weather conditions."

"I had to identify her dead body. I'd never seen that much blood. I vomited."

"It wasn't your fault."

Again the hush of the wide-open desert became the only sound between them.

"She failed you," he finally said. "You deserved to have a caring mother."

Audrey took in several measured breaths.

"I should have been the stronger one at the end. It would have been good for me. Given me closure."

"You'll be an amazing mother someday."

"I know."

While they both kept their eyes forward, she stretched her arm to him and ran her fingers through the jet curls at the back of his neck.

Shane pulled off the road toward the vantage point where they had watched nature's display the first time. When they got there, two other cars were parked. Which seemed odd. That in such a full expanse of desert, two cars would also be at that very spot. Their spot.

He parked, hopped out, opened the door on her side and helped her out of the car.

A door opened on one of the other parked cars. Reg stepped out from behind the wheel. And from the passenger door Daniel emerged.

Connor, Tara and Brittany exited from the backseat.

"What's going on?" Audrey asked, stunned.

Out of the second car, Shane's friend Josefina swung her small frame out. Audrey gave Shane a confused look.

"I asked your father at the brunch today. He said yes."

They looked to Daniel, who was beaming. As were Connor and Tara.

Shane took something from his pocket and then went down on one knee. He held up a simple gold wedding band that glistened under the setting sun. "Audrey Girard, will you marry me?"

"Right here? Right now?"

Her first response was shock but, in a way, hadn't she known all along that by getting in the car with him she was signing on for something?

"Yeah, right now. Will you roll the dice with me, Audrey? Can we ask Lady Luck to give our hearts a fighting chance?"

She couldn't form words. But she could nod her head.

Yes.

Josefina approached. Audrey remembered that she was a wedding officiant.

It was happening.

Not a moment too soon. Shane was to be hers. To walk with. To laugh with. To fail with. To have and to hold.

Josefina gestured to bring everyone close. "*Mijos*, we gather today to celebrate the merger of Audrey and Shane." They all giggled a little bit. "A joint venture. A collaboration. The word *collaborate* means to work with one with another, to coproduce, to join together…"

After the ring was on Audrey's finger and they had shared their first kiss as man and wife, Daniel joked, "Are we working this for a publicity angle?"

Reg pulled out his phone. "Let's take a selfie."

Together, with the open sky and benevolent mountains behind them, they documented the moment.

"That'll give them something to talk about," Daniel said.

"Audrey, my wife… I like the sound of that,"

Shane mused. "Where would you like to go for our honeymoon?"

"I know," she answered big-eyed, pretending to have a brilliant idea. "How about Vegas?"

EPILOGUE

"WELCOME TO MY dining room." Audrey's husband said hello to guests enjoying his Midnight Cakes and Coffee service at Shane's Table Las Vegas. Since the restaurant opened a year ago, a dinner reservation had become nearly impossible to obtain as they were fully booked months in advance.

Audrey had the idea to keep the restaurant open until the wee hours on the weekends for an experience that would let patrons who couldn't get in for dinner indulge in Shane's recipes from his second cookbook, *Dulces Para Mi Dulce*, Sweets for My Sweet. He'd created the collection with Audrey in mind, of course. The hip young crowd that was also filling up rooms at Hotel Girard Las Vegas flocked to the late-night decadence of exotic desserts.

Audrey smiled to herself as she couldn't resist a bite of the piping hot cinnamon-flecked fried churro a waiter brought her to sample. She dipped it into the small cup of accompanying thick hot chocolate while she watched her breathtaking husband charm the entire room. Guests' faces lit up when Shane Murphy, who had reclaimed his rightful place as one the world's finest chefs, stopped at their table to chat.

With the kinks worked out at all of the hotels and restaurants, the Girard and Murphy families had their businesses firmly on course. Reg was back in New York at the moment, moving into a Midtown apartment with his girlfriend Brittany. And Audrey's dad was overseeing a landscaping project at Hotel Girard Key West.

Reg and Daniel were both expected back in Vegas at the end of the month, which is when Audrey and Shane intended to share what they had thus far kept secret.

"The atole is good?" Shane took a break from his hosting duties to make sure his wife liked the rich warm chocolate she was sipping.

"Delicioso," Audrey approved.

"How's our little gamble?" he asked and flattened his palm against Audrey's belly.

"I think we hit the jackpot."

"You know, if her eyes are like yours we're going to have to call her Honey." Shane gave his wife a kiss. "Because you'll always be my Sugar. And life is pretty sweet."

* * * * *

LET'S TALK

Romance

For exclusive extracts, competitions and special offers, find us online:

f facebook.com/millsandboon

⭘ @millsandboonuk

🐦 @millsandboon

Or get in touch on 0844 844 1351*

For all the latest titles coming soon,
visit millsandboon.co.uk/nextmonth